THE
LAST
REDEMPTION

JAMES HOLMES

First paperback edition November 2020

Book design by Adam Hall

ISBN 978-1-7343698-5-4 (paperback)
ISBN 978-1-7343698-4-7 (ebook)

www.jamesholmesauthor.com

"You will die in your sin, where I am going you cannot come."
—John 8:21

"You are from below; I am from above. You are of this world; I am not of this world."
—John 8:23

"You are of your father the devil and your will is to do your father's desires."
—John 8:44

"Hell is oneself, hell is alone, the other figures in it merely projections. There is nothing to escape from and nothing to escape to. One is always alone."
—T.S. Elliot

PROLOGUE

Caesarea Philippi, Judea
29 CE

They journeyed to a place they were not welcomed. What was done here was certainly not part of their way. It was as if he had just stepped off his boat onto a foreign shore, an upside-down land of strange tongues and stranger gods.

The air was hot, and yet as they climbed the stone steps toward the temples, he shivered, as if there was something here in this place, waiting. Waiting to crawl through the rocks and grab hold of him. Waiting for him to suddenly drop dead so it could drag him through the granite into its labyrinth. As they climbed, the stone statues of Pan carved out of the niches in the rocks stared down at him, their eyes hollow and gritty, but still somehow following his every step.

They were not alone. It was bustling with people here to pray to their gods, to perhaps even offer sacrifice to the spring. He watched as a weeping young woman kneeled at the foot of a stone altar and held up a golden bowl toward the goat-legged statue of a man.

For whom did she weep? For whom did she pray, he wondered.

Then he had a strange thought. Was he not cut from the same cloth as all of them? Each trying to find their way.

But as they climbed the stairs, he knew he and the others stood out. He followed closely behind the One who brought them here, because in this strange Babylon he wanted to stay close, even if he could not understand why he was here.

Has He not shown you things you thought not possible?

He has a reason.

You are but a fish in this man's net. And a small fish at that.

They stopped near the top, near the spring that gushed from the cave and He peered over the edge. He shook his head, as if saddened by the swirling waters.

He turned then and spoke to them all. And then He turned and spoke to *him*.

"But what about you. Who do you say I am?"

He could feel the heat now more on his skin.

Who is this man? Is He even a man?

"You are the Messiah, the Son of the Living God."

Their leader smiled. "Blessed are you Simon, son of Jonah, for this was not revealed to you by flesh and blood, but by my Father in Heaven. And I tell you, that you are Peter, and on this rock, I will build my church. And the gates of Hades will not overcome it."

He moved in closer, and as He did, He opened his palm and there, glowing in His hand, was a Roman key.

"I will give you the keys of the kingdom of heaven; whatever you bind on earth will be bound on heaven, and whatever you loose on earth will be loosed in heaven."

Peter nodded. He did not understand the meaning of the words and was far too distracted by the light this man somehow held in the palm of his hand.

As they turned and descended the stone steps, Peter heard a new sound coming from the mouth of the swirling waters.

The chirping of crickets.

CHAPTER I

Somewhere in the Atlantic
40 Days After Event

There was light in the sky, but it was wrong. It flickered and waved, green ghost fingers that turned yellow and radiated across the surface of the earth. It was a gift she thought from God, but she knew it was killing them.

Eve sat on the deck of the boat and stared up at the light show. She looked down at the key in her hand and then to her belly. She wasn't showing yet, but she knew it in was there, growing within, the seed of a dead Roman taking root.

With the ocean gently rocking the boat, the previous night's sleep should have been soothing. Instead, she had a dream that she had clipped off the end of a fishing pole and used the tip, and she'd stuck it inside herself clean and hard, and made a swift fast jerking motion so she could fully slit her womb.

When she woke in a beaded sweat, she wondered whether the dream was a message from God.

What kind of God would want me to do such a thing? To kill a baby.

How can I deny Him?

As she sat on the boat deck, contemplating the previous night's dream, the light dancing above her, she put down the key and picked up the fishing rod. She cut the end off with a pair of snips as the dream had instructed and stared at the eight-inch prod that remained.

Is this what God wants?

Eve looked skyward, but this time she closed her eyes to the light above and spread her legs. The tip hovered just outside of her, and even though she'd done nothing yet, she was already crying. In her mind she practiced what she was about to do, the swift jerking motion, and she moved the tip closer to her body…

If I do this, and kill the baby, I will no longer be pure enough to wield the key.

With a grunt, she tossed the stick into the ocean. There had been no wind, but the sail suddenly flapped next to her as if some unseen giant bird had passed overhead. Inside her head, she heard a dark voice that pushed aside all other thoughts.

Give us the key!

She grabbed the key to protect herself, and it, and as she did it burst into a beam of blinding light that radiated in all directions off the bow of the boat.

She saw then. Everything. What was coming. What she had to do. It encoded into her like a memory.

And she was terrified by what was growing inside her.

* * *

"You alright?" Lincoln asked from behind the helm as she surfaced from the boat cabin.

She nodded, and gave a faint smile, and then looked out across the still water. It was day, or at least his best gauge of day because the sky was the color of lead, and still the lights fanned across the clouds. He knew what it was. The aurora. Which he wasn't sure, because both meant they had drifted too far north or too far south. The temperature didn't serve as a gauge either. It had gotten warmer and the cold that had cloaked them in Philadelphia was gone and instead there was a mist on the water that rose into the sky like prehistoric broth. The signs in the sky were wrong, and he was blinded by the fog, and *if* he were sailing, he would have been lost. But he wasn't sailing, because the wind hadn't blown in days and so they just sat on still water.

He could see the key was already taking its toll on her. As it had Daniel. Her hair was thinning, and she tossed and turned at night, and he'd found long strands of it on her pillow when she woke in the morning. They'd been at sea a little more than a month, but she looked like she'd aged a decade.

He readied the fishing lines, and as he did, he wondered why one of the ends of the poles had snapped.

The fish were still in the ocean, and that made him think God was still in heaven, and an hour or so later, he'd caught a decent-sized tuna, and used the remaining butane to cook it. He set the table for her, and it was becalmed enough to light a candle. It flickered, and he wondered why he was lighting her a candle, but then he wondered if she would know as well.

It was her selflessness that had intrigued him.

How can this be Tom Ferguson's daughter?

He couldn't believe it. It was so surprising to him that someone in her early twenties, a white woman who'd been brought up in private schools and was no doubt privileged, was here willing to sacrifice herself to help save others. Who exactly she was saving, he wasn't sure; she wouldn't tell him. But it impressed him all the same, and like Daniel, the choice she was making was killing her. The radiation of the key was eating away at her, an invisible bite at a time.

"Why do you still need to use the key?" he asked her as they ate the fish. "I thought you said the gate had closed."

"There's something else. Something that crossed. And if I don't keep it contained, it will get out."

"Where's that?" he asked.

"Where we're going," she said.

"What happens if it gets out?"

She shifted in her chair. "Bad things."

She then said she was tired. She was tired a lot and she scooted back the plate of his single fish feast, and he could see she had not eaten much, and she thanked him for the meal. She stood and disappeared into the cabin and he was left to clean up and snub his candle.

* * *

The next night, she was careful again not to wake Lincoln as she tiptoed onto the deck. The air was cool and the water still, but she was sweating already, the white dress clinging to her skin.

She again clutched the key tightly in her hand. It glowed in her palm, and then emitted a blinding white beam. She stepped into the light, and when it dimmed, she was back outside the bunker watching it happen all over again.

Her father was just beyond the chain link fence, screaming at her to hurry up. To run to him. She saw herself, standing there on the other side of the fence, not moving, not knowing what to do.

The driver ran up the road toward her. His gun pointed. The gunshot rang out and the round traveled through the air into her skull.

Her father and the driver exchanged gunfire. The driver fell, her father took a round to the throat. Even then, with blood pouring from his neck, her father dragged her body across the gravel toward the bunker. Toward the place they were supposed to be safe together.

But as she watched him struggling to pull her body, his hand on his throat to stop his bleeding, she knew it was not to be.

He collapsed next to her, holding his dead daughter's hand.

Eve walked across the gravel toward her dying father. She kneeled next to him as he lay there, gasping for breath. It was strange looking at her own dead body next to him, like she was staring at some alien twin.

She wasn't sure he would see her. Even if he did, she had physically changed from the dead girl he now held.

She leaned closer and whispered to him as he lay dying.

"It's Ok," she said. "It's me."

He looked straight at her and tried to speak, but the bullet had sliced his vocal cords.

"Daddy," she cried.

She leaned closer to his ear because she needed to make sure he heard what she had come to say.

"Ask for forgiveness."

He closed his eyes but said nothing.

She wasn't sure if he had done what she had asked. And if he had, if it even mattered.

"Dream of a heaven," she said.

A moment later he died as she held his hand. And even though she had already buried him in her heart, she cried for him again, sobbing in the wilderness as lone flakes of snow gently fell on her, her father, and her own dead body.

She cried not because he had died, but because she knew where he was going.

* * *

A few nights later, Lincoln tried to sleep on the deck, hoping the wind would finally pick up and he could tack to make up for lost time. The wind didn't show. But she did.

She drifted toward him, dressed in her white gown, and he could see she was weak. Her skin was pale, and the dress clung moist to her skin because she was sweating. He swore he could feel the fever heat coming off her body.

"You OK?" he asked as she sat next to him.

She nodded, her lips chapped and cracked like mud flakes, and he offered her a bottle of water.

"Thanks," she said as she took a sip, and then pressed her lips together so the moisture could soothe them.

"What happens when you die?" he asked.

"I don't know," she said. "It's just black. Like I'm sleeping. But there is this feeling of being utterly, completely, alone. Like I'm far out in the universe…abandoned."

"What should I do when it happens?"

"What you're doing."

"Which is what?"

"Taking care of me," she said. She nodded, as if realizing this to be true, and then leaned toward him. A second later she was kissing him, and he was returning it, and even though the boat was still, their bodies were not.

As they lay there afterward, they watched a star streak across the sky. Lincoln knew that the brief burst of orange light that crossed overhead wasn't celestial; it was a satellite toppling from its perch.

"There's another," he said as he pointed.

"Why are they falling?" she asked.

"I don't know. Something must have screwed up their navigation. They're coming home."

She sat up and looked down at him as he lay on the boat deck.

"I'm scared," she said.

"Of what?"

"Of what the key wants me to do."

From there she leaned over the edge of the boat and vomited. He scrambled to his feet, and reached out to help her, and pulled back her hair and stroked her shoulder until she was finished. It felt like such a small gesture, given that she was sacrificing her own body for some battle he couldn't see or understand.

Why won't she just talk to me? Tell me what's happening?

She rolled over and looked at him, her eyes even hollower than before. He handed her a cloth.

"There's something I need you to do," she said as she wiped her mouth.

"What?"

"When we get there…you're going to have to kill me. And I need to stay dead."

He didn't say anything, but his face gave her the answer.

"Will you do that? For me?" she asked.

He slowly nodded, and even though she would be the one to die, he was the one who felt like he was dying.

CHAPTER II

Philadelphia, Pennsylvania
18 Days After Event

The church was a smoking pile of debris, as it had been in his eyes long before it had ever burned down. Longinus rose from the smoldering ashes, near the remnants of the burnt altar. He wiped the flakes of dry, white webbing from his face. The three days had passed, and he had been born again.

He tried to remember how it had happened this time. He felt his eyes, and realized they were still there, and yes, he could see again. He dusted the soot off his jacket and looked around. The families who had raised their guns against them were dead and scattered amongst the pews. Even the children had been turned to ash, their fingers twisted and raised skyward reaching for a mute God, and they no doubt had suffered.

The wheelchair was crushed and pinned beneath a large wooden roof beam, and under it was the charred remains of Daniel.

Fool.

Longinus searched his mind for the only voice he'd ever heard, the One who gave him direction, but he heard nothing.

The walls and roof had crumbled and beyond the burnt trusses were streaks of orange light in the gray sky. Perhaps this was the work of God, he thought. Perhaps, He finally showed, and the invisible wizard had finally used fire and brimstone to smite them and rain his wrath down upon them.

Instead as he stepped into the middle of the street, he saw the remains of what looked like some part of a space station or satellite half buried in the asphalt. It had not been God that had destroyed the church. It had been an instrument of man.

The fool is me.

He moved around it, and saw it was still mostly intact and still smoking, and he looked up, wondering how many more of man's creations would fall from the heavens.

What had the child told him before he died? *Look to the sky, for the figs of men fall.*

As he assessed the heavens, he asked again what he was supposed to do. But the voice inside his head, the One that had long been there watching and commanding, remained silent.

Longinus looked around at the smoking buildings with their windows blown out and at the empty street littered with dead, silent cars.

This is all there will ever be. Even when men are gone, I'll be here, cursed to walk this Earth for eternity. Waiting, for a planet to die.

Where am I to go?

Again, silence.

Eventually, he headed east. To the shore. Toward the only home he'd ever known.

* * *

Sidon, Lebanon

Silas Egin sat on the edge of the bridge, flogging himself. The whip tore through his flesh, each tassel a serpent's bite, and he felt the blood running in rivulets down his back. When done, he placed the whip down and watched the remnants of the damned crawling near him. What had congealed them together had loosened, and now the pieces and parts of bodies had separated from each other and scurried along the bridge like wayward snails.

The smeared faces and parts were still alive, but he knew they wouldn't be for long. They'd bleed out. Starve. Rot. Already the flies had come.

When they died, they would only return from where they came. The pit.

The aurora glistened on the horizon and across the surface of the water. The gray was fading, and he knew. Knew it was over. The One who had claimed him, kept him inside some cell in hell, was no longer inside his mind. He was free from Him. For now.

He had spent his whole life trying to appease Him. This One his father spoke of who had power over this universe. A lifetime spent trying to show Him that he could be worthy of a heaven in hell. Instead, He had taken over his body and locked him in a pit of his own

14

creation. And he suffered there. Over, and over, and over again.

Here now though he had a way out. A way to escape. Because he had the gift to live again.

He knew what was coming in the end. The secret of what lay beyond death was no longer a mystery. There was no one coming to save him. No salvation would be offered. He knew that when the curtain closed, he would only end up again from where he'd just returned.

Hell.

Because that's all there was.

He looked at the rope tied to his feet and to the concrete block he had dragged and rolled down to the end of the bridge. He looked into the water again. It was only about twelve feet deep. Enough to see the sun, if it ever returned. He knew what he was about to do. What would happen when he shoved that concrete block over the edge, and it dragged him down into the sea. His lungs and throat would fill with water, and he would kick and fight and there would be no one to hear his drowning screams. He would look to the surface, at the reflection of light on the water top, and would know there was no salvation. No redemption. Not for him.

Because Silas Egin knew there was no God.

But he said it anyway.

"Forgive me."

He got up and pushed the concrete block, and he fell over the edge with it, and he sank to the bottom. He looked up, the saltwater burning the open wounds on his flesh.

He still hoped some blinding light would part the waters and save him. Some cosmic hand would scoop him up and hold him.

Instead, the saltwater filled his lungs, and seared his throat, and he kicked and spasmed until the will to live was defeated.

He felt a calm as he waited for his brain to die. The darkness that came over his eyes would be the only respite he would know. But it was better than hell.

His last thought before it went to black was that in three days, he would wake beneath the water, and would have to do it all over again.

CHAPTER III

Patmos, Greece
64 Days After Event

The fishermen casting their nets were the first to see the boat anchored about a half mile offshore. It had alarmed them because there had been concerns voiced among Nikodemus and the other village elders that the twisted creatures that had crossed over could rationalize and think, and therefore sail, and it was just a matter of time before a fleet of the damned or the dead showed up and they'd be no match for that. Instead, it was a single vessel. But it was alarm enough.

Nikodemus rowed the small boat through the fog, the oars silent in the water, as two other boats closed in from the other side. The priest sat in the bow. He'd thinned some, left to a diet of mainly fish, but his insides were nonetheless churning his meager breakfast.

They drifted closer and Father Simon scanned the yacht, but all he saw was fog rolling over the deck. He tightened his grip on the shotgun and wondered how many could possibly be on board because he had only four shells, and even though the men in the other boats had crowbars and knives, they would be no match for the size and strength of the things he'd witnessed on the land months ago.

They approached as quietly as he imagined the soldier would have done if he'd been there to lead them. The plan was to scale the sides and surprise whoever or whatever was onboard.

They positioned their boats around the vessel, but before they could breach, old man Nikodemus poked him frantically and pointed. On the deck of the boat emerged a figure in the fog. She was balding, but what hair remained was white as wool, and she was dressed in white and looked like a witch about to cast a spell upon them all.

The priest figured her possessed and lifted the shotgun to his shoulder, but she raised her hands and spoke words he had not expected to hear.

"Church of Patmos. I have been sent to you. I'm here to save the one-eyed man."

* * *

Mara was still too young to crawl, and instead she spent most of her days in her mother's arms in the rocking chair, close to her breast and heart, or in the cradle near the sleeping dog as her mother read from the tattered burgundy Bible.

What she heard from her mother in those early days was the constant reciting of the word. It drifted over her infant ears, a cloak of sounds and syllables she could not understand, but that seemed to soothe her like a lullaby. Good thing too, the woman thought as she looked away from reading and down at the baby in the cradle, because Kat Devier couldn't sing.

There was a moan from the darkness, and she stared into the dark cell at the shadowed man bound to the bed. She'd already changed his catheter, and his feeding tube, and she had sponged him clean. When she did these things, he would stare up at her, his lone eye wide and empty. She would whisper to him that she was here, that she would take care of him, and that he could fight this thing within him.

She hoped he was still there, he had to be, hidden far below the surface. Outside of his moans, and occasional screams, he had not spoken in months. She had wanted her reading to help, but it had shown no signs of doing so, and she wondered if she should just close the good book and abandon it. She talked herself back into it, almost daily, because if the actual words could not heal, perhaps at least the sound of her voice offered him some glimpse of a passing vessel that was still visible from his distant shore.

She cleared her throat again, and returned to reading, when she heard someone at the door. The handle turned and Father Simon stepped into the low-lit room outside the cell.

"Someone has come ashore," he said.

"Who?"

"A man and a woman."

"Are they possessed?"

"I don't know. She knows things. Says she has something. Something to save him," he said as he nodded toward the shadows.

"What?"

"A key that can unlock his cell."

She looked up at the priest, trying to clarify what that meant.

"I've put them in the monastery," he said. "She's asked for you. By name."

Kat again looked to him for some more detail, but the priest nodded and turned and left. Kat closed the Bible and placed it on the nightstand and then leaned down and spoke to Mara lying in the cradle.

"Ready?" she asked.

From the dark cell she heard a low whisper over vocal cords that hadn't been used in months.

"Yes."

The single word chilled her to the core and she quickly scooped the baby. The dog growled at the shadowed figure bound to the bed in the cell. Kat frantically opened the door and called to the barking dog.

"Carrots!"

She yelled for him to come. Now.

Something unseen made the dog whimper, and with that Carrots retreated quickly, tail between his legs, and Kat quickly shut the door and locked it.

It had only been a word, she thought, but one that let her know something was here now, or perhaps had been all along.

Listening.

She stepped outside into the fog and brought Mara closer. Her heart was pumping hard, and as she walked the stone path to the church, there was a thud next to her. She jumped at the sound, her nerves flailed, and a few seconds later, the thud was followed by another.

She approached the sound slowly, searching the thick fog, until she saw what it was. Two birds, doves, had fallen from the sky and lay dead on the stone.

Kat stepped into the small stone-walled monastery chapel where Nikodemus and some of the other villagers watched over their new guests and the priest stood close by clutching the shotgun. As she approached, she moved around the circle of guards, and recognized the man sitting in the front pew.

"Lincoln?" she said. He was bearded and his hair longer, but it was him.

He nodded. "Hey," he said, as if he'd been expecting her all along.

"How…are you here?"

"Well, I…" he inhaled, as if he was about to begin a very long story…

"Because of me," said the woman next to him.

Kat's attention shifted to the woman and she nearly gasped when she saw her. Her face was dead white, her hair in loose strands on her head like she was a cancer patient or radiation victim.

"My name is Eve."

"Why are you here?"

"I've come to help you, Kat. I've come to save John."

"And how would you do that?"

"With this," she said as she held out her hand. She slowly unfurled her bony fingers and there in her palm was an old Roman key with a smooth green skin.

Is this a joke?

"What is that supposed to do?" Kat said.

"Everything."

The woman then told Kat and those in congregation more about who she was, and how she could not die. How she was Tom Ferguson's daughter, and had the pure blood of Belac inside of her, and what the key was able to do. Eve explained that the key was meant for the baby, when the child was older, but that right now she was too young to use it. And so, the task of saving John fell on them.

"How does it work?" asked Kat as she examined the key.

"The vibrations open a kind of door, and when you step through, you can access all things, all places, everything."

"And we can save him with this?" Kat said.

"Not we. I'm not strong enough. You will have to go alone."

"Where, exactly?"

"Hell."

CHAPTER IV

Kat stood over John as he lay on the cell bed. Even though she'd just cleaned him that morning, he already smelled like a wet musky mammal. She half expected him to sit up, to turn or spin his head, to spit pea soup or speak in Latin warning her to stay away. Instead, he just laid still, his body sickly pale and wasting away. He'd lost weight, more than she'd wanted him to, and his legs had not been used in months. They'd been able to repair most of the damage from the shotgun blasts, but the muscles had atrophied. She wondered how much more he could take and if letting him go would be the better way.

She'd left the baby with the elders at the church, and it was just her, Eve, Lincoln and the priest who stood around her in the cell. Father Simon clutched the shotgun, his fingers flexing around the grip, although Kat wasn't sure if that would do any good for what was coming.

"He's still in there," Eve said as she looked down at John.

"How do I bring him back?"

"You will be tempted. He will offer you things. Things in exchange for that," Eve said as she nodded.

Kat looked down at the key in her hand.

"Why this?" Kat said.

"Because it's the only way for them to escape their prison on earth."

Kat nodded. "Great."

"It's OK. You'll be OK. The key will protect you if you walk in the ways of the Lord. But he will erode your faith. If you succumb to his lies, the key will weaken, and you shall remain behind his closed door."

Kat looked at Eve. She would have been twenty-one, maybe twenty-two years old. She would probably have been pretty. Once. Instead the outline of her skull was visible beneath her thinning skin, her lips cracked and bleeding, and she, like John, smelled of dying.

Had the key protected her?

"Remember. When you return. Close your eyes," Eve said.

Kat nodded.

"Ready?" Eve asked.

"I guess."

With that, Kat took the key as she had been instructed, raised it in the air and brought it down hard on the metal bed frame. It radiated in her hands and the sensation wobbled up her arm, and into her skull, until her ear canals shook.

As she looked around, the room in front of her began to fold, like a kaleidoscope of colors being sucked into a black hole. Within a singular space in the stone wall, she watched a hole emerge, and it grew larger.

Kat looked at the people around her, wondering if they too saw this, but they had drifted far from her and were shifting to the color red.

* * *

As Kat faded and disappeared from his sight, the priest stood there, mouth open. What was he seeing? Magic? This woman was disappearing before his very eyes. It suddenly felt like the world he'd known up until this point was only a single pixel of a vast picture, and he'd spent his entire life in that one, tiny, little box.

Had there not been such a quantum and divine display, a true proof of something beyond worlds, he would have seen Lincoln moving closer. But he didn't until a second too late, as Lincoln ripped the shotgun from Simon's hands and then turned the gun on the priest.

* * *

Kat stepped through the dark opening of the prison wall. From somewhere deep within, screams drifted toward her in waves. With their cries, she knew she was stepping into a place out of her control. Her heart fluttered and her bladder quivered, and she wondered if even with the key, there was a way back out.

She turned again, back to the people who had previously been standing next to her. Even though she'd only walked a few feet, they were now miles away, tiny little human dots that stared back at her as if they were looking over the edge of an abyss.

And then they were completely gone.

She was alone.

She continued forward, her chest pounding and her palms sweating as she gripped the key, and looked ahead, down the long, dark tunnel. The shadows on the walls shifted, and she realized then she was not in a tunnel of rock or stone, but inside some giant, writhing hall of bodies, the walls made of flesh. The walls were breathing, and she could feel its thousand breaths upon her.

Keep moving.

She urged her feet to follow her commands, and moved forward, aware she was sinking with each step into the fleshy floor. This was not an illusion, she thought. Not some hallucination. She had been transported to a place that existed on the edge of the only world she'd ever known. As she passed the bodies, she heard them speaking in foreign tongues, and although she could not speak the languages of these dead, she felt like they all asked for the same thing.

Help.

As she moved deeper, the bodies aged, the corpses became more and more decayed until only bone hands reached out for her. It was as if she was somehow descending deeper through the earth, through the sediment of time, past eons of buried dead.

Even as bone though, their whispers remained.

At the end of the tunnel, she saw the flickering of firelight, and she walked up a long stone ramp and emerged into a night illuminated by torches. With the light, she saw the torches were made of humans spired upon spikes, and they writhed and burned.

Then she heard thousands. Not screaming. Not weeping.

Cheering.

She stepped onto a stone balcony that overlooked a colosseum and a crowd. In the center was a giant stone pillar that reached toward the sky, a structure she recognized.

The obelisk?

The one that now stood in the center of the Vatican. On this one though, there was no cross.

I know this place.

The Circus?

She looked below and saw rows of bodies crucified along the spine that ran down the middle of the arena. On the blood-stained sand, a melee of naked people attacked each other with hands and teeth.

A Roman centurion, his face tattered with scars, approached. He stared down at her and smiled.

"The American…"

She looked at him, but did not recognize him, and he gestured with his spear toward the top of the arena. The centurion led her to a balcony where an obese man with red hair sat sprawled on a pallet of pillows. He wore the purple robes of a Caesar, and his beard traced beneath his neck, so it looked like he wore a red-haired collar. He ate meat off a bone, his fingers and face greasy.

Nero?

"We don't get many visitors here," he said as he watched the show. "Our guests, stay."

"This, this is what you look like?" she said.

"For you," he said as he pulled a piece of gristle from his teeth.

"You know why I've come?"

"He is here," the Caesar said as he gestured to the arena floor.

She moved toward the edge of the balcony. On the floor below, the masses had toppled, and John stood naked atop a pile of bodies and battled another naked man. The man was much larger and tackled him and they rolled across the sand. The man bit Sunday and tore away a chunk of flesh from his neck. Sunday screamed and flipped him over and rolled on top and grabbed a human femur, and then beat the man to death with it.

"What is this?" she asked. "Some kind of game?"

"His game."

Only one then was left standing opposite Sunday. And she recognized him. The little mute boy in the blue winter coat stood in the arena. Sunday moved slowly toward the little boy. He grabbed the child and threw him into the dirt and then lifted the bone overhead.

"Please," Kat asked.

The Caesar said nothing, but Sunday brought the bone hammer down repeatedly into the boy's skull.

"No…" Kat said.

When it was done, he peeled off the boy, splattered in his blood, and stared at the mound of bodies and then up toward the balcony.

"Still love him?" the Caesar asked. "When you see his dead?"

She watched then as the circus floor reset itself, like the scene had started over, and Sunday fought the attackers all over again. She turned away and looked back at the man sprawled on the pillows.

"This is all we ever watch," he said as if disappointed there wasn't another show.

"Please," she said.

"Show me what you brought in return."

She looked down at the key in her hand.

"Why do you need this?" she said.

"Because, we have been cursed here for eternity. And He has abandoned us both."

"And so, this, frees you on Earth?"

"Not just. Come and see," he said.

With that, Kat suddenly stood in the valley of a mountain, near the foggy mist of a stream that seemed to flow from the mouth of the sun. She stood in the fog at the base of a giant Baobab tree and watched as six human-like creatures scurried toward her.

Where am I?

As they neared, she could see more of their features. They were tall, with long thin muscles, almost aboriginal, with bushy hair and dark black skin.

The Caesar stood next to her near the base of the tree.

"What is this?" she asked.

"A story you think you know," he said.

She watched as one of the females moved closer to the tree. The mist was clearing, and the bark of the tree appeared to be almost metallic. Its branches were like circuits, and beams of light pulsed and fired in bursts throughout the dark bark. Black pods, almost carbon-fiber in structure, dangled from the branches.

The other primitive humans grunted in warning at the female as she neared, but she nonetheless moved closer. She looked at one of the pieces of dangling fruit, admiring it. A large male stood close by but was hesitant to approach.

"This place was forbidden to them," the Caesar said. "The land of another tribe. But she wondered if there was something to eat here because they were starving from just seed and bush onions. So, she came."

The female plucked the dark pod from the branch and when she removed it, it appeared now to Kat to be more like a large, cocoa shelled fruit, as if it had been this all along. The female squatted on her haunches and took the husk and banged it over and over on a rock until it split. She peeled apart white, fleshy chunks from inside, contemplated it in her hands and then shoved some in her mouth. She continued eating until she had plucked enough of the fibers away to reveal a seed. There she pulled out something green, almost patina. It was round on one end, and looked like it was made of the same metal as...

The key.

The female peeled the key from the fleshy pulp. It glowed in her palm and her eyes went wide and she suddenly stood up and turned and stared directly at Kat, as if assessing her.

She sees me.

Another second, and it was over, and the female was shaken back when she saw a large snake nestled in the roots of the metal tree. The snake slithered toward her. It opened its wide, black mouth and hissed and the female nodded as if she understood, her head almost bowing repeatedly to the serpent.

The female took another piece of the fruit and crammed a piece in her mouth and as she did, the snake struck, and sank its fangs into her calf. A second later, she whimpered and collapsed, and the large male came running to help her. He waved and tapped at the snake with his stick, and grunted at it to retreat, and grabbed the female who convulsed on the ground and dragged her away from the tree.

"Her sin," the Caesar said, "was hunger."

The male pulled her away and stared at her, confused as to what to do. He looked to the others for help, but they were scurrying away, terrified.

He patted at the snake bite, as if this would make it go away. She still held the fruit and he plucked it from her hand and ate it ravenously.

"Did she die?" Kat asked.

"No. But because she was sick, the alpha of the village turned them out." The Caesar nodded toward the male tending to her. "But he stayed with her. And they lived on the fringes of the valley where he nursed her. Gave it all up for her. What was his sin?" The Caesar turned to her. "What sacrifice will you make? For love?"

She looked down at the key in her hands. A second later, she was standing back on the balcony, and she stared down at John on the arena floor. His attackers circled him again. He looked up at Kat, and his shoulders sank, and he lowered his guard. She knew then, this was not just a dream or a game on repeat. He was here and he was aware. Every single time. She raised her hand to him, a wave, a gesture that she was with him. He nodded before the horde swarmed down on top of him.

This time the men tore him apart, and he screamed and cried out as they ripped apart his limbs, and she wiped the tears from her eyes before she turned back to address the Caesar.

"Please…"

"Give us the key. It is the only way. For both of us. We are the ending to all your books. Even now, those who read this, think no such thing as Me exists. We care not. We wait all the same, and when the words are done, we will be there. To collect."

"Some of us are good," Kat said. "There must be another way."

"All ways are here." The Caesar smiled. "I am the beginning and the end."

"No…" Kat said. This thing had to be lying. She couldn't accept that her sum of existence would end in this place. She had tried to be a good person because it had been drilled into her that there would be some karmic payoff. *Was it all for nothing?* Was that why there was evil in the world? Not because God allowed it, but because there was no God to stop it. Humanity was merely a black blossom of this dark root? Was she always just going to end up on the forest floor of the universe, her soul devoured by some cosmic necrophage?

"What you ponder," he said, "is true. You will return. Give us the key, and your place here shall be a palace. Keep it, and we shall consume you for all eternity."

Kat looked to the tunnel and back toward the small flicker of light on the other end. The light of the key in her hand was beginning to dim.

No. She could not part with it. Could not let this thing have it. Could not let it escape. But perhaps, perhaps there was another way. She felt him inside her mind, and they spoke without words.

"So be it," said His voice in her head.

And then she again stood before the tunnel.

"We feed on your hope, your desire for something good," he smiled.

She could see the far end of the tunnel closing.

The Caesar looked to her and smiled. "Do you think you'll make it?"

Kat raced into the tunnel, toward the fading light, and as she did, she felt something behind her. She turned and saw some dark, shadowed figure chasing her in the darkness, closing in on her.

She ran through the flesh tunnel, back toward the light. Ever closer to its warmth. The bodies along the wall grabbed hold of her and held her there and tore at her hair and clothes and begged her with their whispers.

"Please," they whispered.

More hands reached out and held her as the light faded. She yanked herself from them and ran, the tunnel closing in around her, until all she could do was crawl, first on her hands and knees and then her belly, and slowly, slowly, she pulled herself along the floor, her fingers digging into the flesh, until she felt it again as stone...and she emerged into the light as if born again. As she came into it, she remembered Eve's words and closed her eyes and there was a flash so bright she could see it beyond her eyelids.

As the light faded, she opened her eyes, and as her pupils adjusted, she looked around the cell. John still lay on the bed next to her.

Eve moved quickly toward her and suddenly grabbed the key out of her hand. Kat's eyes refocused and she saw Lincoln held a shotgun and pointed it at the priest.

"What's going…"

Before Kat could finish, John shot up in the bed and lunged at her. She screamed as the leather restraints snapped from his wrists and he reached for her. As he did Eve grabbed hold of his arm. She held the key in her hand, and it radiated and glowed in her palm, and Sunday's eyes opened wide. From his body, a dark shadow pulled itself from his flesh, peeled from his very veins, and flowed instead into Eve. It absorbed then into her body, and her capillaries filled with black, and she turned to Lincoln and shouted, her voice sounding like many.

"Now!"

Lincoln raised the shotgun but hesitated.

"DO IT!" Eve screamed.

He pulled the trigger and Eve's head shattered. She dropped to the cell floor, the key still in her hand. Kat and the priest backed away, from both the bleeding body and the man holding the gun.

"Back!" Lincoln shouted. He slowly approached the dead woman on the floor and kneeled next to her.

"What have you done?" asked the priest.

Lincoln leaned in closer to her ear and whispered. "You're not alone."

There was another voice in the cell. This one a hoarse whisper.

"Kat."

She looked over to the bed. His eyes were open.

"John?" Kat said.

He nodded slowly and looked up at her. "Yeah."

CHAPTER V

39 CE-February
Brindisi, Italy

Lucius Cornelius ran for his life. He tucked into the side alley and peaked his head around the corner, trying to catch his breath and see what was coming after him. The fog had crept in off the water and he couldn't make anything out in the murky darkness.

He killed them!

Why?

He heard sandals on the stone street.

He shoved off the wall and raced drunkenly through the darkness.

What happened?

His head was still buzzing from the wine. They'd been drinking with the Roman soldier, having a fine evening. He kept buying them choice bottles, getting them nice and light, when he suddenly pulled his sword and hacked through two of his men like he was reaping hay.

He realized he was running out of road and neared the docks at the end of Via Appia.

What stoked his rage? Something we said?

There was a boat tied near the shore.

Something we did?

As he ran toward it, the soldier who was chasing him stepped from the fog, his sword drawn.

"What do you want?!" Cornelius slurred as he pulled his own sword.

The man approached slowly, the blade catching no glint.

"You," the soldier said.

"Why?!"

"For the rape and murder of my wife in Lanciano."

It came upon him then like a flash of light. The woman beneath him. The murder of them both.

"No, you…we killed you. You were dead."

The soldier was moving closer. Too close.

"And yet here I am to settle the debt,' the soldier said.

Cornelius raised his sword. His running had burned off some of the wine. He was more focused now. Ready to stand his ground.

"Well ghost, you shall die again."

In the fog the clash of metal echoed across the stone street. Cornelius quickly realized he was either still too drunk to fight, or this man was far better with the blade. He realized that at exactly the moment the sword sliced across his face, nearly taking out his eye.

He yelped in pain and then did the only thing he could think to do. He turned and ran. Toward the docks. Toward a passing boat. He dove off the dock edge and into the water and swam with everything he had.

The fishermen watched the spectacle, but then dragged him on board as he clung to the side. Once on board, he watched as they sailed past the centurion who stood on the dock, staring back at him.

The soldier on the shore smiled. A dark smile, like the folly of this escape was but an inconvenience. Then he turned and disappeared in the fog.

CHAPTER VI

Patmos, Greece
30 Weeks After Event

The wind-up watch on Lincoln's wrist vibrated. It was half past two, but in a world without electricity, that was just an arbitrary number he had assigned. It had bothered him at first, not knowing the exact time of day. *1:14? 3:43?* Funny how that minute difference on a cosmic clock still meant a lot to him, and the precise assignment of numbers had given him so much meaning and structure.

It was dark outside, so he pretended it was indeed precisely two-thirty in the morning, and the world outside was normal again. He leaned back, closed his little red notebook, picked up the candle and moved toward the fireplace. He stoked the wood, got a little simmer, and checked the kettle he'd rigged to hang on a crossbar over the coals. The coffee was warm at best, but he still poured it into his mug. It tasted like it had been seeped in a boot, but he finished it in a forced gulp.

He moved down the hall, missing the world and the coffee made by people who knew better, and stopped at a wooden door. He produced a series of small brass keys from his pocket and unlocked the deadbolts he had installed. Locks to keep things out. Or to keep things in.

He stepped into the room and in the candlelight, he saw her there sprawled on the wooden table. She was covered in a thin, white webbing, as if a giant spider had descended in the night to encase her and was still waiting in some corner to devour him.

The candlelight moved over her body, and beneath the stringy filaments covering her face, he could see her eyes were still closed. Her hands rested neatly on her chest and she still clutched the key. Her stomach was still ripe and full. From within there was movement, a little foot or hand that slowly traced the inside lining of her belly.

Her dead belly.

And it was growing. Lincoln pulled the pistol from his hip holster. He knew what he had left in the cartridge, but he pulled and checked it anyway, and loaded the last round into the chamber.

This is it.

After today, there were no more bullets. The island had been able to sustain him, somewhat, but he had scoured it clean and had run out of ammo. He'd found many spent rounds, the remnants of some last stand during the hell crossing, but there were precious few live rounds left. The villagers had talked about an expedition to search out more guns and ammo from the nearby islands, but so far it had only been talk.

That meant in three days he'd have to use the knife. He was dreading that. The gun gave him distance. The knife, he would feel.

He pulled the stool next to her and checked his watch again. Three minutes.

He wondered where she was. If she was watching him from some distant place, the place she had talked about with the key. The place where all things existed. Was she there? Was she with her father? Or perhaps she was with *his* father, and they sat together talking in some garage, while her dad tinkered with lawnmowers or engines.

Then he thought more of his father. About what had happened to him after he'd been fired from the school. How his life unraveled. How his father had fallen from grace after the priest had tried to assault Lincoln.

He looked down at her as she twitched. Perhaps she was merely a prisoner, not in some heaven, but locked in some box in hell by the thing that had come into her. That thought was the one he feared was true. That she was trapped, and all Lincoln was doing now, was prolonging her pain. She could not wake. Could not fight. Just endure in some strange webbed-laced coma, while things unknown tormented her soul.

She shuddered again on the tabletop. He rolled his neck. He'd done this almost 70-times now, and every time, it was difficult. He stood over her and waited. She gasped for air and her eyes opened beneath the webbing and she stared straight up at him, and he knew every time she woke, she was scared because she didn't know where she was.

"It's OK," he whispered because he wanted her to hear his voice again and take it with her wherever she was going next. "You're safe."

And then he pressed the barrel to her temple and blew her brains out across the tabletop.

She spasmed a few seconds, and then stopped. The first few times he'd done this, he'd half expected her to sit straight up and turn and look at him, the white webbing on her face soaking the blood from her skull like cotton and she would ask him.

Why?

Why are you doing this to me?

But she never asked.

He moved over to the corner of the room and picked up the bucket and the marron-stained sponge. He used it again to sop her blood and scooted the little pieces of bone into the bucket. Tiny little pieces of her.

Before he left, he fanned the candle again over her belly. Just to check. Just to see.

He placed his hand on her, which he hated. Because it was not her. Not really. Not anymore. Not the woman on the boat. The woman whose skin he had once felt close to his. The woman who haunted him in his dreams still, because even though they were apart, he had made her into something close. Something he carried with him.

Beneath the white webbing of her belly, he felt it. The baby was most certainly still alive. And still growing.

The knife. He was dreading the knife.

CHAPTER VII

Patmos, Greece
30 Weeks After Event

In the afternoon, the man with the cane and the dog journeyed to the small town nearby.

John Sunday hobbled up the cobblestone path as Carrots stopped to sniff here and there, and he scanned the whitewashed houses. His knees were sore, and the pain carried down to his heels, and he sat for a minute to rest in a patio chair of a long since abandoned café.

He stood again and adjusted the strap on the shotgun. Lately, his weapons-runs had diminished. He'd already pillaged all he could find, and kept it hidden away. This trip was different. He wasn't looking for guns.

The houses were empty, and he moved on to the shells of the stores and strolled past like he was window shopping. Past the T-shirt stores he found the small shop he sought, which had long ago sold their wares to the tourists and pilgrims who once came to this island. The store shutters were still closed from the hell winter that had come and as he and the dog stepped inside, it was stale and streaked with shadows.

He searched the small glass display cases, wiping away the coats of dust so he could peer inside. There were dozens of rings still in the cases. They had no worth in this new world and were just stones again. There were big, fat, glittery rings with price tags he never could have afforded on a soldier's pay, but even now he thought they were too much.

He settled on a small band, one with a stone that wouldn't get in the way of cleaning fish or gardening, and he plucked it from its red velvet nest and tucked it in his pocket.

As he stepped toward the storefront door, something rustled in the back of the shop. The dog bristled, and Sunday turned and brought the shotgun around, and there on the back wall was a shadow. It was small, distinctly human in form, and it seemed to stare at him as if it possessed eyes somehow in that darkness.

Then it moved.

It wasn't from some shifting cloud outside. IT moved.

Then, he saw what he had not seen since the winter. Something *unknown*. The shadow stepped off the wall. It the size of a child and its little shadow arms reached toward him as if looking to be embraced. A second later it was if it had skipped through time, and it had covered the length of the room and stood inches from him.

This shadow he knew. He couldn't see anything more than blackness, but he could tell.

It was the little mute boy he had killed.

But this time, the little mute boy wept and whispered.

Help me.

The dog barked and the shadow retreated slowly into the surrounding darkness. He did not flee, but merely seemed to return.

Sunday stepped out into the daylight and he and the dog left the child confined to the shadows.

* * *

There was crying.

Am I dreaming?

Sunday woke and sat up on the side of the bed. He looked over at Kat sleeping in the darkness next to him. He reached out, felt for the lighter on the bedside table, and flicked it until he lit the wick.

There was another cry, and for a moment he remembered the sounds of the pit. The dreams were worse at night, and when he woke it took him awhile to figure out what was real and what was not.

There it is again.

Mara.

He slowly got to his feet, his bones still stiff. Sometimes he felt like the creatures watched him sleep, or followed him around the room, and leered at him from the shadows. He had to tell himself repeatedly they weren't there, like he was a child again working up the courage to look for the monster under their bed. As if to mock his logic, his mind would play tricks on him, and the walls and doors would seem to breathe, and the shadows would lurch like they were trying to reclaim him. His hold on reality had turned fragile, and he was certain of precious few things anymore.

He looked at the cane next to the bed and opted to go without it. He hobbled past the sleeping dog, who gave him no notice, and over to the crib in the corner and looked down at her.

"Hey," he said. "What's wrong?"

She was sitting up and looked at him and reached her little hands toward him. He picked her up and brought her close to his chest and held her there, to soothe her, but she wouldn't quiet so he walked into the kitchen so he wouldn't wake Kat.

He laid her out on the table, and changed her diaper, and talked to her as he did. He told her that she was stinky, and he pretended to be offended by what he'd found in her diaper, and she smiled at his little side-show. When he'd finished, he picked her up and she was calm. She would start walking soon, and he'd have to find a new way to keep her even closer to him.

He held her and moved toward the front door and stepped into the night. The lights in the sky above were awake as well. The colors of the aurora flickered and tickled the sky, but it was what was beyond that took his breath away.

He'd never seen that many stars before. There was more white than black. He could make out the dust of the Milky Way. He was no astronomer, but Lincoln knew the stars and they had stared up at it on many occasions together, and Sunday had learned their names as he had pointed out things and asked questions.

"Somewhere, beyond that dust, is a black hole," Lincoln had said. "And we, and everything else in this galaxy, circle it. All of us bound to it. All of us revolving around a destroyer of worlds."

Lincoln had told him that the view made no sense. This was more than just the elimination of all light pollution because the electricity was gone. This kind of stellar clarity, Lincoln said, meant something was wrong. He believed that whatever had crossed, that had pumped dark chimneys into the skies, had somehow affected the atmosphere. And because satellites were falling, and they were seeing the aurora at this latitude, the magnetic fields had been affected as well.

The result though was one hell of a view.

And Sunday wondered as he peered up, if something else peered down.

He also worried about what he'd seen in the store. Whether it was real, or if the things that had haunted him since the coma, were more glimpses of a brain gone mad. Or that perhaps something was really out there still waiting for him.

Mara fussed a little in his arms, and he brought her closer to his chest, and then beneath the heavens, he started to sway.

He sang the Joe Cocker song he knew she loved.

He didn't know all the words, but he repeated what he knew with some of the rhythm, and he swayed there with the baby beneath the cosmic canopy.

Kat came to the doorway and watched them dancing.

He saw her there, and he nodded for her to join them, and then with the baby between the two of them, they swayed together. As she rested her head on his shoulder, and Mara played with Kat's hair, he dismissed what he'd seen in the store and instead thought that they had finally made it. Together.

* * *

She looked at him as he stood there with her, dancing beneath the stars.

He paused for a moment, and seemed to take her in, and she felt self-conscious, because she had just woken up, and her hair was a mess and her breath likely bad. He gave her a small smile, and even though his face was scarred, and his eye gone, he was still there.

For him to stop and stare and look at her still meant something. She felt something inside, a love for him that had grown into something different, evolved as she watched him care for a child that was not his. Evolve into the man she had always thought he could be. She smiled. Awkward. Self-conscious. It was meant to tell him that yes, it would be okay.

A second later, he adjusted Mara and sat her down gently on the ground near his feet. He reached into his pocket and at the same time pulled in her hand and then kneeled. He presented a small ring as he looked up at her.

"I don't know what time we have left. But you are, and will always be, the only way in my heart. Will you marry me?"

He was a man of few words. But what he said choked her heart, and even though the ring he had found didn't fit, his love for her did.

* * *

Father Simon married them in the stone chapel of the monastery. John and Kat stood with a lone audience of

Mara playing on the floor near their feet, and the priest spoke of a world beyond that lives in their hearts and watches them with more patience than the shadows that see the same. A world that some doubt but is true because each of us seek an emotion unnecessary in the void that exists nonetheless: love. To be quenched by it, to be accepted by it, and this love is the key to that kingdom beyond.

"And in this way, we seek redemption from the universe, from each other and from ourselves. To know that we are connected.

All children come from a broken home, but alas, you shall be collected into His house, and you shall know that you are welcome.

And although the world and many souls have been stripped of this hope, there is a place where all ways are the way, and love is a force that carves gravity and time. And in this place, you shall be my last disciples."

Father Simon delivered the words.

And he was proud he had done so, because the words were strong, albeit cryptic. He watched them kiss, and he looked down at Mara as she played.

What Father Simon did not know was where exactly those words had come from. It was from no sermon he'd ever heard. From no book he'd ever read. The words came from his mouth, but he was not sure where the thoughts had come from.

Mara looked up at him as she played on the floor.

And she smiled.

CHAPTER VIII

Caesarea Maritima
39 CE-March

Cornelius had used his uncle's rank and pull, accepted the transfer and taken the ship. He stood on the boat deck as they arrived in the bustling seaside city. The limestone lighthouse in the harbor was blinding in the morning sun, the water glistening ripples.

Once they docked, he was escorted by the soldiers toward his uncle's home. As he came down the stone path toward the house, he was surprised to see his uncle loading food in a wagon for a family. A family of Jews. Despite his age, his uncle was doing much of the lifting and loading of the crates.

As the family's cart lumbered past him, his uncle stepped toward him and they embraced.

"Look at you! You bear the signs of a centurion!" his uncle said as he patted the scar on Cornelius' cheek.

"Aye," he said as he watched the Jews depart. "Is this what you do with your food here? Give it away?"

"To feed others, is to feed oneself," his uncle said. "Come," he said as he put his arm on his shoulder and escorted him into the house. "Tell us about your journey."

That night in the courtyard, by the light of the fire, Cornelius' uncle listened to the tale of the soldier who had seemingly returned from the dead.

"I tried to stop them. Stop them from attacking her," he said, "but could not." He knew this was a lie, but he could not bring himself to tell his uncle of his deeds. Besides, what mattered here was the dead man who had returned. "He killed them all. And now he comes for me."

His uncle eyed him, and Cornelius wondered if the deceit had worked. His uncle then leaned in, stoked the fire and sipped from his cup of wine.

"This story," he said as he sipped. "It bears semblance to another I've heard."

His uncle told him of a crucified Jew who had supposedly risen from the dead. "They preach now, some of them, that he is their messiah, returned from the dead."

"Nonsense," Cornelius said.

"Why then," asked his uncle, "does a Roman soldier a shore away also appear to have the same skill? Perhaps there is some magic here we do not understand."

"Is that why you help the Jews?" Cornelius asked. "Do you believe this?"

"I believe that I tire of the ways of Rome. There is only ever too brief a peace between bloodshed." He reached for the bottle of wine. "I seek something more...filling."

"Do you not provoke the gods?"

"Perhaps," his uncle sighed. "Or perhaps if I don't do these things, I provoke theirs."

Cornelius stared into the fire and sipped on the wine and the words. He noticed the altar in the courtyard and saw it had been stripped of any plates or incense.

"Where are the offerings?"

"These Jews," his uncle said as he leaned back, "Preach something else. Something I find most interesting." He sipped his wine again. "Something *you* may find interesting."

"What's that?"

His uncle leaned closer, so the fire revealed more of his face.

"Clemency."

CHAPTER IX

Patmos, Greece
38 Weeks After Event

"She's possessed!" shouted one of the fishermen at the village gathering in the monastery chapel.

Some of the others echoed the sentiment, which for once had been said out loud instead of whispered.

"The devil is in her!" cried another.

"If it is born, what came, will come again," preached Nicodemus from the front of the church. "The only way to be sure is to burn them! BOTH!"

Sunday stood in the back of the church, near the priest, and looked to Lincoln who shifted nervously.

"Who are you to decide?" Kat stood up and asked. "To decide the fate of this woman or a baby?"

"You see it! She's a dead woman! And yet the baby within grows!" Nicodemus growled.

"It does. And does that not seem like some kind of miracle?" Kat said.

"A curse!" shouted another.

"There comes a time when God puts his dark deeds in the hands of men," said Nicodemus. "This is that time!"

"What do you know of dark deeds?" Sunday said from the shadows.

The elders and villagers turned. They knew the man with one eye spoke little, and because of it, the crowd was hushed.

"Any of you ever taken a man's life? Heard him cry for mercy? Used a blade to slice a throat, felt his pulse on your fingers? All you've ever done is catch fish."

"Killing that thing will be easy," said one of the fishermen sitting in a pew.

Sunday pulled his fishing knife from his hip and handed it to the man.

"Go then. Do it. Slice the baby from her belly."

The man looked at the knife in Sunday's hands, but then lowered his head.

"Perhaps you know what she carries," said Nicodemus. "Because it was in you. And you wish to protect it."

Sunday smirked. "You think I'm trying to save her? I'm trying to save you all," he said as he pointed with the knife.

"This is a price we are willing to pay," said Nicodemus.

"Then let me explain again," Sunday said. "If such a thing were to happen to her, then I will do the same to those who have done it. And then you will know dark deeds."

* * *

On the day of the birth, Kat didn't know what to expect. No one did. No one had ever delivered a baby from a dead woman.

When it came time, the signs were still there, and there was a pool of liquid on the tabletop between her legs. Lincoln had fetched Kat and the others, and the women and handmaidens filled the small, planked wood room and watched. Kat looked down at the cocooned woman and she shivered, as if something else was there with them, watching them from the shadows.

One of the elder women acted as the pump, and she pushed upon Eve's white-webbed belly, while another propped her up from behind, and pushed some more. Kat moved between her legs, and pulled away some of the white webbing, and watched and waited.

"I see it!" Kat called.

They pushed more, and Kat saw the crown, and she reached in and held it firm, and then it was there, and she caught it in her hands.

And so, he was born.

Another second and she cut the umbilical, and then she looked at the baby. He opened his eyes and cried. She examined him closely. Looking for, for... she didn't know what. He was just a boy, Kat thought. Like any other.

* * *

Sunday held Mara as he and the priest stood outside in the hall, while Lincoln paced, and the women tended to the pregnant woman.

Sunday looked to Lincoln when they heard the baby crying from within.

The priest said a prayer, "May God bless you and keep you in the name of the Father, the Son, and the Holy Spirit," but as he spoke, the baby in the other room cried even louder.

"Healthy set of lungs," Sunday said to Lincoln.

As he spoke, there was the sound of a large thud outside. Sunday stepped to the doorway and saw a pelican had fallen on the stone path. It struggled to lift its head, flapped a moment, and died.

Mara began to cry in his arms.

* * *

Hours after the birth, Father Simon was at his writing table and put down his pen when he heard a knock. He raised the candle as he opened the door and saw Lincoln standing there. Even in the candlelight, and even though he was a dark-skinned man, his face looked bone white.

"I need to confess something," Lincoln said as he shifted his feet on the porch and held his cap in his hands.

"Come," Father Simon said as he opened the door wider.

Lincoln shuffled into the little stone house and sat on a small stool near the fireplace. Father Simon pulled up his chair next to him.

"Tell me," the priest said.

Lincoln looked to him. "It's not what I've done, Father. It's what I'm about to do."

"And what's that?"

"I'm going to kill her. Permanently."

"Why would you do that?"

"You know why. Because there's something inside her. And if it gets out, what happened before will start all over again. So, I'm leaving for Ephesus. It's where she told me to go. Where she told me to do it."

"What about the child?" Father Simon asked.

"Well, she wants you to care for him."

Father Simon shifted in his seat. "I'm an old man. I'm no good with children."

"She said you'd say that. And she said to tell you, this…this is your penance."

"For what?"

"For the children you left to Father Zula."

Father Simon paused and stared at Lincoln. "How do you know that name?"

"She saw things, man. Things that have been done. Things that have yet to be done."

Lincoln stood and started for the door. He turned back before he left.

"So, am I forgiven?"

"I don't know. I don't know what God wants anymore," the priest said.

"Yeah, that's what I figured."

* * *

While the village slept, Lincoln checked his little red notebook again and did as he had been told. He stole Eve's body in the night and the key she still clutched in her dead, white-webbed hands. He carried her spindled corpse to one of the boats and then rowed to the yacht still anchored off the coast. He pulled her on board, the stars and the aurora their only witness, and then set sail.

When he arrived a day later, he docked the boat and dragged her onto the shore and rested her body near a fence post until he found a wheelbarrow near a construction site. From there he wheeled her to where she had told him to take her. He left her leaning against a stone pillar and went back to the worksite, loaded up on the supplies he needed, and wheeled it back. In all it took four trips to get everything.

He made the box out of pine planks, and although he was no carpenter, he was impressed it was fairly square. From there he dug the hole, and the ground was mainly lime and rock, and it took work to break it and he swore it was getting hotter. He checked his watch again, although she was his only ticking clock.

He needed water, and he found a hotel nearby with a swimming pool. The water was brown and murky and would have to do for the job, so he filled two five-gallon buckets and then carried them back. He then searched out more buckets from houses and sheds.

There were still bodies scattered in the streets, and some in the homes. The freeze had preserved the flesh longer than it should have been so that all this time later, there was still decaying skin on the bone and the smell of rot in the air. He came across an old woman still sitting on a bench, still plump in death, her flesh black and flaked. He half-expected her to jump up, like the things he'd seen in Philadelphia, and run screaming toward him. Instead, he ignored her as he hoped she did him and searched until he found enough buckets and jugs to do the job.

He placed the pine box in the hole, and then her in the pine box, gently as he could, and he was careful to make sure the key still rested on her chest. She lay there in the little wood box and tried to discern what new face had been built for her this time. Beneath the white webbing he couldn't make out much and he imagined there was no face at all, and she was just embryonic flesh with no eyes or ears. Even in the heat, that image in his mind of her face pale and blank, sent a shiver down his spine.

He laid out a tarp and mixed the sacks of concrete with the shovel, adding water as he went. Then, a shovel at a time, he dumped the concrete on top of her. He started with her feet, and then filled that area, and worked his way up her calves, and thighs, then her waist. When she was half encased, he paused, the guilt heavy on him because he worried this wouldn't work, and she would wake nonetheless, alive for a terrifying few seconds over and over again every three days, before she suffocated again. He continued, and made sure to really pack the concrete tight, so there would be no air pockets, nothing but concrete around her. No way for her to move.

He shoveled in more, until her chest and the key were covered, and then came the part he dreaded most. He paused with the shovel over her face, and held it there, as if she'd suddenly wake and sit up and wonder again what he was doing to her. He turned the blade, and the mix rolled off the shovel and onto her face and he continued until the box was filled.

When it was done, he sat near the pit, and as promised by the instructions on the bags, he tapped on the concrete within an hour and it was hard.

Hours later, he looked at his watch, and the alarm vibrated, and he leaned down close and listened to the concrete box. He half-expected to see the concrete shake, or to hear some faint scream, but he saw and heard nothing.

He finished by shoveling the dirt and filling in the hole, and then he patted it down, and he wondered if what they had done had worked. He contemplated making some kind of cross for her grave.

Instead, he cleaned the site, and left her unmarked except for what she had left in his heart.

That night, under the glare of a torch, Lincoln found the other site she had told him about. He knew it from his history books, but it was also marked for tourists and pilgrims--now history themselves. He walked through the remnants of the once grand entrance to the church, and he remembered its name: The Gates of Persecution.

What he sought lay in the center of the stone columned ruins of the basilica. Around it were a few solo pillars and partial stone walls, all that was left of a church destroyed by earthquakes centuries ago.

Because it was getting hotter, he had decided to work at night. The sky above him flickered green and yellow as he laid out the tools he would need.

He pulled down the lone rope barricade and looked down at the site and wondered. It was roughly 15 by 15 feet. How thick was the marble? How much rock was below? How long would he have to dig?

Is he even down there?

He read the stone marker: The Tomb of St John.

Well, that settled it.

If the marker said so, it must be true.

Lincoln raised the sledgehammer above his head, and it landed in an unremarkable imprint on the surface of the tomb.

It took every night for a week.

On the seventh day, his shovel hit something hard. He worried it was more rock, and all he'd done was for naught, but he decided to be tender with the shovel blade just in case. Eventually he got down on his belly and cleared enough dirt away so that he could make out a solid stone surface below.

Under the light of the rising sun, he dug out the edges, and then wedged a pry in along one side. He cranked the pry and was able to lift the lid and look inside.

My God.

She'd been right. The bones were stacked neatly in the ossuary box, but there was something else with them. He reached in, and as he touched it, he was afraid. Afraid that by disturbing it, he'd trigger something that could not be undone.

He grabbed hold of it anyway, and strained as he pulled it out, and looked at what he held.

It was a book. Bound in either calf or sheepskin, it weighed easily twenty pounds. He could see the book was perhaps two to three-thousand pages thick.

Don't open it.

That's what she'd told him. Not that he could. On the cover, were seven metal straps. They weren't chintzy, but solid, almost titanium-looking, like something used to hold a ship or bridge together. The metal looked modern, a stark contrast to the ancient book. The clasps were connected to a single lock buried in the cover of the book.

As he looked it over, he realized this wasn't a book written by a disciple in the first century. It certainly wasn't sealed by one. No. This book was *given*.

Given by someone from another time or another place and buried in a first century tomb.

He wondered what was inside. Perhaps it was just some ancient cookbook. Or original copies of the gospels.

Or perhaps some alien lord had given the cheat sheet to the universe and it contained all the answers to all the questions.

He checked the lock again. Lincoln was fairly sure there was only one key that could open it and he had just buried it beneath six feet of dirt and concrete.

* * *

A week later, he sat in the abandoned house he had moved into and re-read his notes. He checked a map and searched for the location she had told him about on the voyage across the ocean. He found the street name she had given him, and then traced out his route.

He hid the book under the bed, and again wondered about its contents. He'd contemplated digging her back up, chiseling the concrete, and taking the key from her spindled grip. In his hypothetical, he'd unlock the book, just to see. See if he could read the text. See what the gods had to say.

Instead he packed and set out again and navigated the streets, and the interstate, following the lines. He was near the end of the map, when he saw it.

Down the end of the street, there it was. Just like she said. A used car lot.

Lincoln strolled across the parking lot, half-expecting some overly aggressive Turkish used car salesman to come out of the front office, ready to make a deal. He searched the cars, until he found what he was looking for. It was in the back, hardly showcase ready. The tires were flat, the leather seats peeling, the once shiny metallic paint now coated beneath a layer of dust. There she was though, just like she'd said. A Mercedes 240D. If he had to guess, he'd say she was circa 1981. He popped the hood and as soon as he did, he smelled that old grease and grime, and he was back in the garage with his father. Working on an engine again. Lawnmowers, weed whackers, an occasional motorcycle. But his father loved working on the big engines the most.

"Diesels," his father had said, "never die."

Those were the days he missed. When his father was in control of his temper and they would just talk. His dad could bring any engine back to life.

Lincoln disconnected the battery and the alternator. Then he changed the flat tires. He siphoned gas from a few other diesel trucks and filled the tank. He knew he'd have to search out more gas containers and collect more fuel, so he'd have enough for his eventual journey, but for now he had enough to get home.

He pushed the Mercedes toward the downward slope of the lot. He pressed down the clutch, put it in gear, and slowly rolled down the hill. A few seconds later, he released the clutch, and the engine started. A few minutes after that, he was cruising along, for the first time in months, the wind in his hair, the rattle of the diesel in his ears. He hadn't been behind the wheel in a long time. Hadn't felt the engine of man in a while.

He felt like a king.

CHAPTER X

Patmos, Greece
39 Weeks After Event

The villagers clung to their beliefs on the boy. He was pre-judged, and perhaps would have been cast into the sea, had it not been for Father Simon.

The priest couldn't blame them. The boy had come from a dead mother, whose corpse had disappeared right after his birth. Feeding the baby was the immediate challenge. Kat was the only one on the island producing milk and so she had volunteered to feed him. She took him, and he screamed in her arms, but the sound triggered her instincts and the milk was there, but he would not drink.

If he didn't eat, he would die. So, the priest and Sunday scavenged for options. The island had been home to only a few thousand people, most now dead or gone, and they searched homes and found only one with a canned container of formula in a cabinet. It was white powdered gold, but it would not last. Father Simon knew where they could find more milk, but such a notion would only add to the villager's superstitions.

Days later though, as the last scoop scraped the bottom of the tin can, the priest set out and climbed the hillside below Chora, and he saw them there. They fed as if the freeze and the hell had never been. The island had been known for its goats, and they grazed on the grass and the tree leaves until they spotted the priest.

He did not know if it was curiosity or hunger, but the goats approached as he stood in the rocky field, and he spotted a plump, hairy female, her udders low. She drew closer, and looked up at him with yellow eyes, and he slipped the rope around her neck and guided her back down the hill as if she'd been waiting for him all along.

Father Simon understood why the elders and some of the others feared the baby. They were simple folk, and many had lost loved ones, and narrowly survived the hell coming, and so their fear guided them. The priest knew though what he had to do. He had failed the other children, failed the mute boy too, and by his count as a priest he had lost more than he had saved in this life and he wondered if his cosmic calculator would ultimately come up short.

He brought the goat down from the hills and into the backyard near his small stone house, and he milked her, and then took the crying baby from Kat. The priest readied the bottle, and the goat milk was still warm, and the baby took it and drank. As he looked upon the child, he felt despite the circumstances surrounding his birth, he needed a fair shot and the priest would give him such a chance.

He rocked the baby in the chair and the priest knew the child needed a name. He wanted a good, Christian name, one innocent enough so not to draw any more attention. Matthew, Mark, Luke, John. He settled then on a perfectly fine Christian name.

"Hello Jacob," he said.

CHAPTER XI

Caesarea Maritima
39 CE-October

Even in the crowded market, Cornelius heard their whispers.

As he passed the temple, he nodded toward a group of Jews lingering outside. He wished nothing more than a simple gesture in return, but an older woman in a tichel ran up to him, hands extended, drawing even more attention to him.

"Good sir, thank you, thank you for the alms for the temple. May the Lord bless you and keep you."

He nodded, but he turned to the shopkeepers and customers across the way. They were talking about him and stopped and stared.

He understood their eye. What had he become?

Here he was, wearing the armor and colors of Rome, and while he paid allegiance to Caesar, he no longer worshipped their gods. He'd been raised to pay homage, to offer sacrifices on holidays, to seek the guidance of his ancestors. To make offerings before and after battles. He had turned his back on all of it.

He was still Roman. Still a centurion. But his heart had been filled with a different light.

Now he wondered what would happen if one of these Jews, and one of those shopkeepers had an altercation. What would he do to keep the peace? Would he hurt another? Would he again draw his sword?

That was not the way.

Not his way. It couldn't be.

Not anymore.

* * *

That afternoon, he retired early and knelt to pray in the domus. Their customs were still new to him and he struggled with their words. He had not learned their formal prayers, and so, made up much of what he said from what he heard in his heart.

"Please, Lord, forgive me."

He closed his eyes, and when he opened them again, he was blinded by a striking white light that nearly seared his eyes. He fell backward and scurried toward a corner. There, in the middle of the room stood a man who appeared as if he'd just pulled back a curtain. He had a broad face, large nose, and short black hair. Around him it was blinding, as if he wore robes made of light.

"The way to me is through you."

Cornelius cowered in the corner and shielded his eyes from the light.

"Seek a man named Simon, who is called Peter," the man said. "Together you shall loose the earth to heaven."

* * *

As he rode from Joppa to Caesarea Maritima, Peter did not know why a Roman centurion had sent two men to retrieve him. But he feared the reason. As he rode in their carriage, a stranger seated near him, he reached his hand into his pouch and touched the key.

He closed his eyes, and felt it there, wondering if the key would show him another vision as it had the day before. He worried he was riding toward the same centurion who was there at the execution of his Lord. The one the key had also shown him, the one who would one day lead him to his death.

Is that day today?

"Are you well?" asked the man sitting in the carriage with him.

"Yes," Peter said as he opened his eyes. "Just tired."

As he entered the centurion's home, he was immediately greeted by a man with a scar across his face. Almost as immediately, the man fell to Peter's feet, weeping. Peter was stunned.

"Stand," Peter said. "I am only a man."

The centurion rose and nodded and wiped his eyes. Peter looked around the atrium, where several others stood.

"This, you must know. It is against our law for me, a Jew, to visit with you," Peter said.

The centurion nodded but seemed not to care.

"I am Cornelius," he said as he sat and gestured to the chair across from him.

Peter did not take the seat. "Why is it you have called me here?"

"I have seen a messenger of the Lord. In this very room. He said to seek you out."

"*Who* told you this?" Peter said.

"A messenger," Cornelius repeated. "Bathed in white light who appeared to me here, as I prayed."

Peter looked around the room. There were others standing there against the far wall, families with children, who nodded at him as if they too knew this to be true. He wondered then if this was some sort of trap, and soldiers hid in the wings, waiting to arrest him. If the Pharisees had rounded the Romans to do their biddings and they waited only to hear his words so he would indict himself.

"And what else did this messenger say?"

"That you are Simon Peter, and I am to travel with you as you preach. That only then can my past sins be forgiven. That I must follow you in the way."

"The way is not for you," Peter said.

"The messenger said you would say this. That am I not a Jew. But it is why he showed you a vision. Before I called upon you. A vision that as a fisher of men, you must not throw the rest of us back. What God has made clean…"

"You must not call profane." Peter finished. His mouth dropped. The key had shown him this, and told him this, and he had not fully understood what he had seen. He looked closer at the centurion, gauging his face. "What else did he say?"

The centurion nodded toward Peter's pouch. "That you carry the keys to the kingdom, and with it, all worlds will be one."

Peter nodded again. He did not understand what was happening or why. But he did know one thing.

"That messenger who visited you," Peter said, "was our Lord."

That evening, Cornelius waded into the shallow waters of the impluvium in the atrium of his domus. Peter waited there, and Cornelius kneeled before him.

Peter spoke then, and the centurion closed his eyes. When he did, he saw her. The woman they had attacked. She was beneath him, begging for him to stop.

Peter cradled his neck and tilted his head back, and he felt the water flow off him. As he did, he felt the memory of her washing with it.

What he had done, had been lifted from his heart. He felt the Lord God had forgiven him, and he would lead his life now in the way.

He hoped then the Lord would also stop the man who hunted him, because he would not be as forgiving.

CHAPTER XII

Lanciano, Italy
Four Years After Event

From beneath a large-brimmed hat, and covered head to toe in cloth, Longinus rested against the handle of the shovel. He took a breath, the hot air harder to take in, and from beneath his goggles he scanned the field. There was nothing he could do.

It was all dead.

He had come home and had worked his family's land once more. He'd even planted olives again, the first time in two thousand years he'd attempted the crop. He figured he'd have plenty of time to see them mature, and perhaps they'd grow old together. The first year after the winter, the plants took. The melting ice from the hell freeze had left the soil moist enough, and even though the sun had not fully emerged, and the skies were gray, there seemed to be enough light filtering through to get the roots to take. Soon he had shoots, then stalks, then trees.

For the first time in that two-thousand years, he looked out at his field and saw he had grown something again on this land. He had turned the barren soil into fertile ground and within five years he expected to see his first olive crop. But then the light came, this time to burn.

It was subtle at first. The gray skies receded, and with it he saw the sun again. He had not realized how much he had missed the warmth on his face. The problem then were the rains. There weren't any. There weren't even clouds. Spring and autumn had come, and the rains had not, and the earth cracked and the ground turned to dust.

He stole water from a lake seven miles away, and had done the most Roman of things, and constructed an aqueduct out of pipe. It kept him busy, and when it came time to pump the water, he felt nothing but joy to see it pour onto his arid land. He had conquered it he thought, and his crops would win.

He was at peace. Back on his father's land, the sun above his head. It had been four years since he'd heard the voice of the One. Without it, a quiet had come upon him.

Occasionally, as he retired on the porch, he saw her sitting there next to him. He had even put two rocking chairs out, and as he rocked, he imagined Licinia there stepping up behind him, sitting next to him, their wrinkled hands clasped together, a touch no time could take.

But it was not to be. And she was not there. And he was alone.

Eventually the light began to bake. The days grew longer, until most of it was just day, and the skies were so clear he wondered if the sun had moved closer in the heavens. If he went outside, even in the short night, he could feel the radiating heat on his skin, and he'd be sun-burnt without ever seeing the sun.

He knew why, or at least he had an idea. No plan had ever been divulged to him, but he knew the earth was dying.

He knew this was a sign. The beginning and that in the solar sanctuary above his head, the Morning Star would return to reap a Venus upon this land.

CHAPTER XIII

Patmos, Greece
Four Years After Event

Someone was talking to Mara from the shadows of her room, and it was not her mother or father.

That night, after her prayers, Mara climbed into bed and her mother and father kissed her good-night and then retreated to their bedroom with the candle. They left the door open, as they always did, and although the candlelight had faded back down the hall, there was movement near the doorway as the shadow shifted.

Mara sat up in bed.

"Hello?" she said.

And with that, the someone appeared in the door-way.

The shadow whispered to Mara. They whispered in the old words and Mara spoke back in them.

They talked for some time about what was to come.

* * *

Kat woke from a dead sleep because she heard voices in the house. She sat up, startled, and didn't bother to light the candle, because she knew for sure it was coming from Mara's room.

She moved quickly down the hall, in the darkness, and she heard Mara speaking, but then also what sounded like a very faint, whispered response.

She moved into the room and saw Mara sitting up in bed. There was no one else in the room. No one she could see.

"Mara, are you OK?"

"Yes mommy."

"Who were talking to?" Kat asked as she moved closer to the bed.

"My Invisible Friend."

"Who is that?" Kat asked as she searched the shadows.

"She told me to tell you, it's OK. It will all be OK."

Mara laid back down in bed and then rolled over. "I'm tired Mommy. Love you."

"I love you," she said as she sat next to her on the bed. Kat stayed with her for some time, watching the shadows to make sure there was no one else in the room. Perhaps, in another life, that once would have been a quick scan and she could have gone back to sleep. Now though she lived in a world where things she never imagined were possible. The key had shown her that there was but a curtain between what humans see and don't see, and that it wasn't man who had the power to pull back the cloth. There were things out there, on the cusp, and she often stayed up nights wondering if what the Caesar, the lord of lies, had told her was true: that he was the beginning and the end.

Finally, she returned to her own bed. When she did, John stirred next to her.

"What is it?" he asked, his words slurred with sleep.

"Mara was talking to someone."

"Someone in the house?" he asked, more awake now.

"No…I don't know. She called her, her Invisible Friend."

"That's normal."

Kat laid down and stared up at the dark ceiling. "No. It's not."

John rolled over and looked at her in the darkness. "Why?"

"She was speaking in Aramaic."

* * *

When the short nights came, and the sun wasn't out in full force and scorching the sky and the ground, Mara and her father went fishing. Her mother covered her head to toe to protect her skin from the rays, and then slathered on sunblock like she was painting her. Mara and John walked down to the dock, just the two of them, and they set out in the boat where they would sit and fish and talk.

On this night the sun had just set, or as much as it set anymore, for the night now was nothing more than a four-hour sunset. Mara had brought the two toy dolls her father had found on one of his scavenger missions to the other islands, and she sat on the deck of the boat and played. As he unfurled the sail, she pretended the dolls were mommy and daddy. She made them dance together, and the mommy told the daddy that she loved him, and the daddy said it back and John was pleased that part had been conveyed into her translation.

She switched then to what seemed a more intense conversation.

"It's so hot," Mara said as she spoke as the mommy doll. "Why is it so hot?"

"It will be OK," she said in the daddy doll's voice.

"Everything is dying. What are we living for?" said the mommy doll.

"Each other," said the daddy doll. Then she spoke in her own voice. "Don't worry. We'll save them."

That part of their conversation piqued John's interest.

"Who will save them?" he asked her.

She looked up at him and smiled. "That's what she says."

"Who says? Mommy?" he asked.

"My Invisible Friend."

"Who is that? What does she look like?"

"I don't know," Mara said.

"You don't know?" he said.

"She doesn't have a face. It hasn't been made yet."

John shifted near the stern. *A woman without a face? Is this Eve? Somehow talking to Mara? Is she alive?*

"What else does she say?"

"She tells me things," she said.

"Like what?"

Mara looked up and smiled. "Everything. And she wants me to tell you this."

"What?"

"That I am the One."

Sunday looked at her, and she smiled and went back to playing. John leaned against the mast, watching her, wondering what that meant. Wondering if it was good or bad.

When they reached the fishing spot, she put down the dolls, and helped him with the poles and baited the lines, and the two of them sat there, nothing nibbling the line, but with plenty biting in John's mind.

He sat and stared at her as she fished. He had known for some time she was special. She had an understanding of the world that exceeded her years. Father Simon said she knew the Bible backwards and forwards, but more importantly, she understood it. The big words, and the old words, didn't matter. She and the priest spoke often. And if Lincoln had still been around, John suspected she would have talked to him too. About the stars, or black holes, or time and space.

As they sat in the boat, the fish were absent, as had become more of the norm. The sun was on its way back up, and when it rose it would be far too hot, and there would be no more fishing that day. The fish would descend to the lower depths, seeking some shadow that could shield them. He would be forced again to return empty handed, the village reserves already running low, and some feared they had survived being frozen in the hell winter only to be burned alive or to starve in the eternal summer.

He moved to the net and folded it again so he could toss it in hopes it would catch what the line had not.

He wondered then if he would watch Kat and Mara die, and if he could keep his faith if famine claimed the ones he loved.

Mara turned and looked at him.

"We will feast in the New Jerusalem," she said.

"What?"

"But to be together, you must be saved."

She turned then and looked at John, and for the first time, he felt nervous around her. His hands trembled as he clutched the net.

"Daddy, turn fully so that your sin may be cast."

He looked at her, at his little girl, trying to understand who she was.

"What are you saying?"

"Look," she said as she nodded to the rising sun on the water.

He turned and faced the sun and felt its warmth on his face. There on the horizon he could see dancing light and in that bright light he saw a vision. It appeared to be himself, standing there, surrounded by blinding rays.

"What is this?" he asked.

"The way to me is through you. This is the moment of redemption. Ask *it*."

John Sunday stood on the boat, the sun upon his face, and closed his one eye and he asked for the thing he had felt he could not. He had planned on waiting until he knew for sure there would be no more killing, and he would no longer be its killer, and then perhaps he could plead for forgiveness. Instead, the judgment came to him on this boat, on a random sunrise with his daughter staring at him. He kneeled then and saw there was a carpenter of the cosmos, and he had weight and worth, and that it loved him. He felt the words then, not in his brain, but in his heart, and he lowered his head and asked the unknown:

Please. Forgive me.

When done, he opened his eyes, and she was close to him and she whispered.

"I love you," she said. "I have cast your sins, again."

"I love you," but by then he was crying, and he didn't know why.

She smiled. "It's Ok daddy. Go ahead," she said as she nodded to the net in his hands.

He tossed it into the water and watched the weights sink it, and then collected the ends to pull it on board but by then he could feel its weight change. He looked to her, because he knew the net was full without even dragging it aboard, and she smiled.

"And so shall be your heart," she said.

CHAPTER XIV

Patmos, Greece
Seven Years After Event

The priest raised the boy as best he could. As he grew, he read the Bible to him and Jacob was tuned to every word. The priest found him a peaceful child, and he played softly and gently, and showed no signs of being anything but a little boy. Jacob and Mara were often together, and there was no friction, and they played as children should.

One day, just after his seventh birthday, Jacob was playing in the backyard as the priest lounged in a near-by patio chair. Father Simon had been working to repair the fence for the goat, and it had gotten too hot, and he laid down his tools and sat to rest but instead fell asleep beneath his straw hat. The boy played with his wooden blocks and built them up, and then knocked them down again. The priest fell asleep to the sound of toppling wood, and when he woke again, he was standing in the delivery room where the boy's dead mother was giving birth.

It did not feel like a dream, but instead a place he truly was, and he watched as Kat and the other women massaged and pushed on the webbed woman's belly. Beyond them he heard whispers in the shadows, but there was no one else he could see in the room. The women squeezed and from Eve's corpse came a splattering. Because the women were in the way, the priest could not see what was happening, but then the women gasped and backed away from the table.

The priest stepped around as larvae and insects and maggots rolled out of the pregnant woman and tumbled off the sides of the birthing table and onto the floor. Then something else emerged from her dead body. It was black and furry, some kind of wet rodent-thing, but on top of its head was a nub ring of horns.

He took a step back as the foul thing came onto the table in a rank spill of blood and fluids. The whispering around him became louder, and the baby made a deep guttural cry like a bellow, and then he heard it again.

The sound of the crickets.

The creature squirmed on the table and bellowed and cried. He feared then that what he was seeing was what had truly been born, and this thing had twisted their visions and what they saw instead was a little boy, when it most certainly was not. And he was deeply afraid.

He woke to the sound of the clinking of wooden blocks and looked down at the little boy who played in his yard.

Jacob looked up at him and smiled.

It was not a menacing smile, but sincere.

Sincerely what, the priest did not know.

Three days later, Father Simon found the back gate open on the new fence he had built. He dressed to cover himself from the sun, and went out and called for the goat, and shook her feed bucket, but there was no response.

He traipsed down to the bottom of the hill, and over another, and that's where he found the goat. Her neck had been broken, and sickly twisted backwards, and he thought she had taken a fall, which he thought was rare for goats. He kneeled in front of her and saw then her black fur was stained with pockets of blood. He touched her and his fingers slid into an open wound in her skin.

This was not a fall.

He crossed over another hill, and then saw them. Dozens of goats splayed in the field. All of them dead.

In a nearby patch of hawthorn, he kneeled and picked up a screwdriver. His own tool that he had used to mend the fence. The tip was coated in blood and still had strands of fur stuck to it.

The priest looked back up at his little house on the hill.

"No, no, no," he said out loud. He had tried so hard to give this boy a home, he thought. A place of love. To defeat any notion that evil was born instead of bred. As he clutched the screwdriver, he was afraid. Afraid that what the boy was could not be stopped, and he wondered now if the boy knew he was down here, and this had all been done just so the priest could find it.

So, I would know.

The priest's gut bubbled and his heart felt heavy with guilt and grief. He crossed back over the hill and looked down again at the goat who had once suckled the boy, and thought she deserved a proper burial. Instead, he trudged back toward the house in the cursed heat, contemplating his role and responsibilities as a father, and whether he should discipline the child. He had never raised a hand to the boy, and instead followed the root meaning of the word discipline, which was born from disciple. And like them, he sought to lead, in hopes the boy would follow.

As he crossed up and over the threshold of the hill, he saw the boy standing there. Waiting.

It was then the priest realized if there was a disciple here, it was him.

* * *

Under the cover of the short night, the priest packed up their items, what was of necessary value, and loaded it onto the fishing boat. He told no one they were leaving, and he and the boy set sail for one of the abandoned islands that decades ago had housed prisoners. Father Simon knew what the boy had done with the goats would only be kindling for the villager's fears, and so the priest had to do what he could to keep him safe.

As the priest rowed the boat, and the island drifted from their view, he wondered if the boy minded that they were leaving the only home he'd known. The boy answered his question without speaking.

"It doesn't matter where I go."

CHAPTER XV

Ephesus, Turkey
69 CE

Cornelius was tallying a ledger in the back room of the small sanctuary and heard someone call for him from the front.

"Presbyter?"

"Come," Cornelius called. He looked up from his writing at two gray-haired men who stood in his doorway. "How may I help?"

One of them, a man with a long beard and well in his eighties, nodded.

"You are Cornelius, the centurion?" the old man asked.

"I am Cornelius, the overseer of the way here."

"I am Lazarus."

Cornelius looked up from his tally sheet.

"May we speak?" the old man said.

Cornelius stood and quickly scooted some papers off a nearby stool. "Yes, please. Come, come."

With the help of the other man, Lazarus groaned from age and sat. "What I wouldn't give to see Him again," he said as he nodded his appreciation to the man who had helped him.

"Blessed be our Lord," Cornelius said.

"You traveled with Simon Peter?" Lazarus said as he adjusted himself to be more comfortable.

"Aye, for many years we preached the word together. Before I settled here."

"And in that time did he speak of the other centurion? The one who executed our Lord."

Cornelius could feel the heat flush his face. He had not thought of that man for many years. He *nodded*. "Aye. We spoke of him."

"Then you know he cannot die. And he has again taken from us," Lazarus said.

"What?"

"The Key." He leaned forward. "You have seen this?"

"Yes," Cornelius said. "When Peter held it, I saw things I never knew existed. Visions beyond my understanding."

Lazarus looked to the other man in his sixties standing in the doorway.

"This is John. He was there the day of our Lord's death."

"You…you traveled with our Lord?" Cornelius asked.

The man nodded. "I too have seen the power of the key," John said. "The day our Lord took me up the mountain, and he held it in his hand, and I was blinded by its light. I saw the door of the kingdom swing wide, as if it opened from the sky. When it did, I saw myself as an old man in a cave and He stepped out and handed me a book. I could not read it, because the cover was locked. But inside I knew it contained the revelation of ourselves, of all of us. It was the story from the first man and first woman to the last. All that we are, all that we have done, all that we will do. From this, all shall be known, all shall be judged. And it could only be unlocked with the key."

"What could the centurion do with such knowledge?" Cornelius asked.

"That's what worries us," Lazarus answered. "To wield the key, you must be one with the Lord. Like you, he followed in the way for many years, until he fell off the path. The threat though remains that he could somehow use the key. It belongs with us. With true believers."

"What do you seek from me?" Cornelius said.

"Find him. Find the key. We shall hide the book when it comes to us, but the key must be taken from him," Lazarus said.

"Me? Why me?"

"Because you too are a centurion. A man who has done terrible things in his past, yes?"

"And this qualifies me?" Cornelius said. "Look at me. I am an old man. He is a man who cannot die!"

"We know nothing of this. You. You have killed before."

He slowly nodded, remembering. "Aye."

"Then we beseech you," Lazarus said. "Time is precious. A follower of the way in prison saw the centurion wield the key with Paul. He watched then as he cut off Paul's head! The centurion has seen what the key can do. Hunt him down. Take it from him!"

"And how am I to do that?"

"Return to your sword."

Cornelius shook his head. "Nay. That way is long dead to me."

Lazarus leaned in. "Trust me, Cornelius. What is dead, can come back."

CHAPTER XVI

Lanciano, Italy
Seven Years After Event

In the mid-day sun, nothing could be done in the fields, so Longinus sought other things to occupy his time. He was clearing out the cellar when he stumbled upon the old paintings. The portraits of the dead painted by Mary Magdalene so many eons ago. He picked up one, a painting of a girl no more than twelve with fine black hair and wide eyes. She had always given the eyes so much focus, so much vision. He assessed the painting, one of the many he had purchased through the years in an effort to find what she had hidden beneath the paint.

For the first time though, he saw it as something different. Something beautiful.

He took up painting shortly afterward. It took him some time to scour the neighboring houses to find some hobby painter kit, but when he did, he set up under the shade of the front porch and went to work.

Before he laid brush to canvas, he closed his eyes. In his mind, littered as it was with the debris of time, he could still see her face. Not as it was when she was suffering from the men who had attacked her. Not as it was when she was dead or had been flayed in the pit. But as she was when the sunlight hit her face, and she looked at him with love in her eyes, for that vision was still sacred in his heart.

He began to paint her then, the canvas his new field, and her face upon it the only fruit he wished to grow.

Eventually, the riders returned. They rode hard, the dust a wake to his memory, and he wondered if he were still in the pit all along. The horsemen neared the porch, and he could see they were Roman soldiers, and he wondered again if time was playing tricks in his mind. But as he saw his optio Tiberius step from his horse, he knew it was not the past and present that had jumbled in his mind. It was the One who had returned and was speaking again to him.

Tiberius stared at the paint-smeared smock that Longinus wore and looked to the painting where Licinia was there, upon the canvas.

"Not bad," Tiberius said.

"Not good either," Longinus said as he wiped the paint from his hands on his apron. "What do you want?"

"Rome has need again."

"Have I not fulfilled my duties?"

"One last ride Centurion. One final time before you, and all of this, ends."

CHAPTER XVII

Patmos, Greece
Seven Years After Event

John Sunday came from the docks and headed toward the small house on the hill. The dog lay near the door, his ribs showing more, and Sunday wondered at what point Carrots would die and if they would be forced to eat him.

He took off his headscarf, and sunglasses, and hat and boots and stepped inside. He was weak, down to only a few hundred calories a day. He stepped inside as Mara played on the floor in the corner, while Kat salted some fish at the kitchen counter. Mara jumped to her feet and ran to him and clutched his leg.

"I missed you daddy," she said.

He kneeled in front of her, the effort to get down and back up again exhausting. As they hugged, she felt thinner too.

"I missed you."

He sat at the table and Kat brought him over a plate. There was a small slice of fish upon it. He looked up at her but said nothing. Her face was gaunt, her eyes unusually wide and round, the skin shriveling up around them.

"I'll go out farther tomorrow."

"And then what?" she asked.

"Then we'll see."

"The water is too hot. All the fish are dead."

"They're just deeper. I'll use more line."

She turned away from him and went back to the sink. John looked down at Mara who played with her dolls.

He pushed the plate away and walked over to Kat as she washed a pan in a soap bucket. She scrubbed it, hard.

"It's so hot! Why is it so hot?"

"It's going to be OK," he said as he reached for her hand.

"Everything is dying," she said as she shook him off. "What are we living for?"

"Each other."

Kat shook her head. She looked down at Mara and lowered her voice. "Is this…is this, what all this was for? Seven years of surviving…just so we could," she paused, and lowered her voice to a whisper, "so we could starve?"

"We won't starve Mommy," Mara said as she looked up from her dolls. She stood up and walked toward her mother. "But we will die."

"Why are you saying that Mara?" Kat said.

Mara looked up at her mother. "Because Mommy. What is coming, is the way."

CHAPTER XVIII

Gyaros, Greece
Seven Years After Event

Father Simon watched as Jacob slept near the crackling fire that he had built inside the abandoned brick prison. It was dark here, cold even, but it was at least a respite from the scorching heat that baked the outside. He wondered if they could make it here. If there were goats on the island, because he had seen some of their bones on the way in, so perhaps there were more and they could sustain them. He hoped.

As the boy slept, he watched him and worried. He'd only ever sought to bring this child peacefully into the world. But on the boat ride over, the child had spoken *in his mind*, and he wondered if he was still in there now, tinkering around, reading his thoughts, knowing what he was going to do before he even did it.

The child shifted on the mat next to the fire, and with it, the flame sparked and sputtered as if suddenly alive.

It was then the priest heard something else moving in the shadows. He stood and saw him there, just beyond the light of the fire. Another child. This one he hadn't seen in a very long time. It was the boy from the church basement in Poland. The one he had failed to save. He cowered near the flame, frail and naked on his haunches, his eyes wide with fear. Father Simon looked at him, and as he moved, the priest could see something dangled from his backside. The priest squinted to see better, and there he saw it. A crucifix that had been inserted inside the child's rectum, and when he moved it dangled from him like a tail.

No...

The boy crossed around the fire, closer to Father Simon, and it was then that he realized the child was circling. Coming closer.

No. It's not real.

But as he thought it, he looked and saw the boy left footprints in the sand, and a second later, the boy grabbed him and pulled him close and Father Simon knew then this was no dream.

"You left me," the boy wheezed. *"Do you know what he did to me?"*

The priest felt his heart tighten in his chest and he violently grabbed hold of the boy in fear and desperation and yanked him off and threw him into the fire.

The naked boy stood then upon the embers, his body burning. But he made no sound. The priest had no weapon and even if he did, he wasn't sure it would work. Not against this thing that stood in the fire. Instead, he ran, and even though he'd lost plenty of weight, he could feel his heart and lungs bouncing inside his chest.

He raced through the hall of goat bones, and as he did, they came to life and their skeletons nipped at his heels.

He ran out of the prison, squinting in the scorching sun as he made his way toward the shore where he dragged the boat down to the water and clamored over the edge and started to row. He rowed fast, fast as a fat man could, and when he was far enough from the island he looked back.

He saw Jacob standing there on the shore.

A little boy. A little dot of flesh.

He slowed on his row, and then he considered that perhaps he was just going mad from starvation, and that he had just left the little boy alone. He thought he should turn and go back, but before he could, he felt his heart seize again. This time it was like an invisible hand that gripped his chest and squeezed. He grabbed at his heart, to release the grip, but instead he sunk lower into the boat.

He panted, hard, trying to catch a breath in the infernal heat, but it wouldn't come.

Just one…good breath.

As he seized, he saw Jacob at the front of the boat, crouched like a crow on the stern. He looked down at the priest and smiled. A dirty, naughty smile.

"Show me," Jacob said.

And with that the priest could feel the boy inside his mind, and images were there before his eyes unspooling like a film reel. All of it. The war in Lebanon. The priesthood. The boy in the basement in Poland. He saw himself sitting in a room again with Lincoln and they were speaking about where he was going, and suddenly it was all over.

Then, and even though they were on the ocean, hands burst through the bottom of the boat. They shattered through the wooden hull, and were long, and stretched, like bone tentacles and they grabbed at Father Simon's feet, and he kicked at them.

"NO!" he screamed. "Let me be!"

But his heart was hurting so much he couldn't muster much of a fight, and the hands grabbed hold of his legs, and before he knew it, he was dragged through the floor of the boat, through the wood bottom, and the hands pulled him down, down, down into the deep, deep, dark.

CHAPTER XIX

Patmos, Greece
Seven Years After Event

John Sunday headed out early again that morning in the boat, before the baking heat, and caught enough of a breeze to carry him farther out than he had been on previous trips. The wind was hot, by his guess the air temperature around 120, and he had to tuck low in the boat to prevent the breeze from burning his skin. He moved slowly, the heat melting away any extra energy, the moisture peeling from his body before it could even pool on his skin.

He looked to the sky, before the sun had risen for the long hot day and saw there was still some faint remnants of the aurora there. On the distant horizon then, he saw them, like a black cloud.

Birds.

He headed toward their winged circle, but as he got closer, he could see they were in a frenzy. They flew up, then down, and some fell out of the sky. There was land in the distance and when he neared it, he loaded the shotgun and anchored the boat close to the shore. He waded through the surf, and there were birds standing near the waves, but hundreds more littered the sand with their carcasses, and some crashed down around him as he emerged from the sea.

They were geese and all white, and he presumed they had been on some kind of migration. They seemed way off course, and he wondered if this was where they were supposed to migrate to, or they were just falling out of the sky from sheer exhaustion. One was on the ground, still breathing, panting wildly, and severely injured. He kneeled and watched it struggle for breath and remembered Mara's warning again that they were all going to die. He wondered if God cared about dead birds more or the same as dead people. He reached down and held the bird's head and neck gently between his fingers, and then yanked hard.

He adjusted the strap on the shotgun and picked up the bird from the sand and grabbed a handful more that looked freshly dead and carried them back to the boat. He tossed them in, then went back for more, because at the very least he figured they could salt the meat and turn it into jerky. The birds were thinner than the average goose, and he presumed they had burned off their reserve fat long ago, but there would still be enough meat to feed the village.

Sunday looked skyward again, and wondered how long this sky feast would last, and he figured they'd have to return with more boats to pack the rest before all the useable meat just rotted on the shore. As he watched the birds, he saw something else on the horizon. It was faint, but there.

Smoke.

Sunday crossed through the shriveled remnants of thistle bushes toward a crumbling red brick prison. Some of the windows still had bars over them, and he saw the smoke coming out near a rooftop.

He tightened his grip on the shotgun and stepped into the dark corridor. His boots crunched gravel as he moved down a hall littered with the scattered remains of goats; their horns curled on top of their peeling skulls.

From somewhere at the end of the hall, he thought he heard voices. They were somehow familiar to him, even though he could not understand the words.

There was dander in the air, and squawking, and when he moved around the corner into an open room, he saw him lying there on the sand of the old prison floor next to a dying fire. The priest. Father Simon.

His fat gut was partly flayed and ripped apart as crows picked at his flesh. He'd been plucked apart for some days, yet his body looked freshly wet, his skin water-logged and loose and the sand around him wet, as if he'd just been dragged here from the sea moments ago.

Sunday shooed the birds from the body and they squawked, their cries like laughter.

He kneeled next to Father Simon. They'd been through much together. The journey to Sidon. Their time together on the island. He had baptized Mara. Presided over his vows to Kat. This man had taken him in, into the church when the hordes had first come during the hell freeze, and he had likely saved his life.

He was more than a priest.

He had left, Sunday presumed, so he could protect the boy from the villagers. They'd not spoken, but Sunday figured he'd do the same if it were his child.

Sunday called out into the shadows of the prison.

"Jacob!"

No response. He checked the prison and called out as he searched the dark cells and found no sign of the boy.

He returned and assessed the priest again, and decided he would have to drag him outside, bloated and ripe, so he could bury him.

He spent the next few hours tracking down a shovel and digging the hole. It was exhausting in the heat, and when he finished digging, he barely had enough energy to tie a few sticks together into a cross for a feeble grave marker.

He dragged the body, still heavy even though he'd lost plenty of flesh, and scooted him into the hole. He then filled it back in, and with the heat taking so much out of him, when he was done, he lay near the mound. He'd wanted to say something, to bless him with some prayer, but he could only muster a single word.

"Please."

Please forgive him for his sins. Please protect him from the things that devour the dead, that lay in wait for the final pat of the shovel on the mound of men's souls. Please carry him to heaven. Please let there be a heaven.

Please.

When he was done, and he'd scoured the island again looking for the boy, he returned to the shore.

Except his boat was gone, and as he scanned the horizon, he saw no sign of a sail.

He'd been duped.

CHAPTER XX

Patmos, Greece
Seven Years After Event

The boy arrived on the shore the next morning. At first the fishermen on the dock paid no attention to the boat that drifted through the mist, and presumed it was John Sunday returning to port. When the boy emerged from the boat and stepped off though, Nicodemus and the men stopped working their nets and lines and turned and stared.

Some stood ready to confront the child, and Nicodemus grabbed his fishing gaff to end this once and for all.

"Dark deeds," he muttered.

The boy dragged a bloody bird by its neck down the dock and tossed it in front of him. Nicodemus looked down at the boy.

"Tonight, we feast," the boy said.

Nicodemus looked to the dead bird, its neck sickly twisted, its eyelids wide and its pupils rotting. Despite its appearance, he was certain he could smell its sweet juices cooking on the fire.

* * *

That night, Kat stared out the window of the little stone house. The villagers had turned out at the monastery down the hill and smoke billowed from the chimney. She smelled the aroma of cooking meat drifting up from the village.

What are they doing?

Are they eating without us?

She looked over at Mara who was sleeping in the bed, the dog at her feet. She quietly opened the door and slipped off into the fleeting darkness, driven by hunger.

She moved quietly down the cobblestone until she came to the chapel. From behind the closed door, she heard whispers within. Whispers that reminded her of the ones she'd heard when she was in the cave all those years ago.

She turned around, half-expecting to see someone standing behind her, because she was certain someone was looking over her shoulder. There was no one there. She turned back to the church door, her palms sweating as she reached out for the handle. Suddenly, she stopped as she remembered the Caesar's words: *her sin was hunger.*

What are they doing in there?

Kat crossed instead to the side of the church and traced up and under a window. She peered in and she could see them, their bodies twisted in the frosted glass.

They were distorted plumes of flesh, but still appeared naked, writhing and bowing repeatedly. They stood and kneeled again and again, their pale skin twisted and congealed in the church glass window, and others danced and bowed and she heard them whispering something unknown from within.

They faced toward something, something shadowed sitting in a chair near the altar, but she couldn't see exactly what. In the glass, it appeared dark and furred, like some kind of bear or beast. She turned to get a better angle, but as she did the dancing stopped, and the naked bodies slowly turned around and stared out at her.

Her gut sank. They knew she was here.

She ran back up the cobblestone path toward her little stone house, and quickly closed and locked the door.

As she caught her breath, she wasn't sure what she'd seen. Why she'd even run. Was she hallucinating because she was starving?

Mara was still sleeping, and Kat double checked the lock, but she knew it would do little if they were to come.

Please. John. Come home.

She couldn't wait. She rushed to the bed to wake Mara so they could escape into the night.

Mara sat up in bed and her little feet touched down on the cold stone floor. Kat went back to check the window. Some of the villagers now stood in the yard, while more were coming up the stone path.

Mara walked up to Kat and reached out and held her hand.

"When it comes, don't be afraid," Mara said.

Kat looked down at her. "They are not going to take you."

Mara nodded toward the window. "They are many and we are few, as it has always been."

Kat kneeled in front of her daughter. "I won't let them hurt you."

"What I say mommy, is that I am here to protect you. And in the end, we shall be clothed in the light together."

She looked down at her daughter. "Mara, are you saying we're going to die?"

"Yes."

* * *

The villagers stood guard in the yard, while the vertical wooden posts went up sometime during the night. The morning mist clung to the bases, although Kat knew with the coming of the sun, the fog wouldn't last long.

Kat clutched a frying pan in her hands and guarded her post at the window where the villagers stood like crows on her lawn. Even in the fog, she could still see some held crowbars and axes. At dawn, she watched as Nicodemus moved toward the house. It was happening.

He clutched a fishing gaff and lightly tapped the metal hook on her door, like he was about to sell her something.

"Kat," he said gently. "Sorry to bother. Would you mind coming out?"

From under the bed in the back bedroom came a muffled voice.

"Mommy, this won't stop them."

"Shhh."

A second later, Kat jumped as something loud slammed against the front door. There was another whack, and another, until the wood splintered, and Kat raised her lone frying pan in her hands.

Old man Nicodemus kicked the door from the jamb, and he stepped through the door. She threatened him with the pan for a second, and then went for the strike and brought it down on his forearm. There was a snap, but he made no cry. He grabbed her with his other arm, and she tried to bring the pan back round again, but he punched her hard in the face and then ripped the pan out of her hand. She was stunned from the blow, but before she could recoil, others quickly stormed into the house and grabbed her. She flailed and hit at them, but one of them knocked her to the floor and they kicked her.

"NO!" she screamed as Nicodemus stepped past her and into the darkness of the bedroom. He kneeled next to the bed and looked down at Mara.

"Hello Mara."

"Hello Jacob," she said.

* * *

They dragged Mara and Kat out of the house and into the yard. It was there they pulled and stretched their arms behind them and tied the wooden patibulum around their elbows. Mother and daughter were kicked, and pushed, and dragged back to their feet and led down the hill, toward the monastery, toward the two posts driven into the dirt that waited for them outside the walls.

"It's going to be OK," Kat cried to Mara as they were laid out flat on the ground. Nicodemus moved over her with a hammer and long spike. Another of the fishermen took Kat's arms and stretched them wide.

"Please," Kat begged. "Don't."

Nicodemus looked to the church as if waiting for an answer. The dark entrance stood wide. There was no one there she could see, but Nicodemus nodded nonetheless. He readied the spike near her ulnar artery and raised the hammer.

A second later, he drove the spike in, and Kat screamed.

CHAPTER XXI

Gyaros, Greece
Seven Years After Event

Sunday scoured the island for another boat but knew it was a long shot. No one lived on the island. The tourists who came to see the abandoned prison, and dive off the shore, came here only by boats that turned around and left when the tour was over.

As he searched, his mind was racing. He knew the boy had taken the boat. Perhaps the boy had also killed Father Simon. And now he was headed back where? To the island? To Mara? To Kat?

He found no vessel and stood alone on the shore, the birds falling from the sky around him, and stared out at the horizon.

How far?

Ten, maybe twelve miles.

That's just to the nearest island.

He was in nowhere the shape he used to be. He was weak from lack of food. He didn't know if he'd make it. Then he heard her voice in his head.

Daddy.

They're here.

She was as clear as a whisper in his ear that made the hair stand on the back of his neck.

He kicked off his shoes and stole the laces and used it to tie the shotgun to his ankle. The surf was hot as he waded out, the shotgun dragging behind him, and he started to swim.

As he swam, his mind focused on getting to them, but his body was already betraying him. He was too weak, too exhausted, too starved. He had to command his body with each stroke.

One arm in front of the other. Go. Move.

He wasn't sure he was even swimming straight, or if he'd been pulled off course by some current and he'd just miss the island entirely.

The shotgun was dragging him down, pulling at his leg, tugging at him as he…

It's not the gun…

There was something there. Pulling his foot.

A shark?

No, this wasn't nibbling.

It's pulling!

Something yanked him and then dragged him beneath the water.

He fought to surface, but it pulled him completely below, and there in the deep he thought he would see it staring back at him. There was nothing there. Nothing he could see tugging on the shotgun, but he quickly struggled to untie the lace from his ankle so he could free himself and surface.

Then he did see. The ocean floor far below was open and wide, a chasm of fire, and inside were shafts of molten lava bubbling to the surface. The ocean bed had cracked.

The earth was broken as far as he could see.

And there were things down there. The dead creatures of the hell freeze were swimming out of the crevice toward him. They looked like human crabs, their limbs stretched out, fingers clawed and spread wide. Reaching. Reaching for him.

They were closing in as he was pulled down toward them.

Down into the abyss.

He struggled to untie the shotgun from his ankle. The surface of the water just above his head, not that far…but it wouldn't let him go.

I can make it.

His lungs filled with water, and he was starting to seize. He couldn't escape. He began to surrender.

It's over. Be free.

He closed his eyes, and the saltwater entered his lungs, and he knew he was drowning. They were coming for him because he was dying. They were there to claim him.

Then he saw them in his mind. Kat and Mara. They were huddled together on their knees and the village elders were standing over them. He could tell they were scared. In the vision, Mara turned her head toward him, and she whispered to him once more.

Daddy. Please.

And he surged, and snapped the lace that tied the shotgun to his ankle, and the gun sank toward the abyss and he lunged back up, and kicked, not sure if it was a death spasm or the will to live, to fight, and he pushed off the water, pushed off the invisible thing dragging him down…and he…fought…and…

Surfaced.

The air, scorching, yet he took it fully into his lungs and it burned as he inhaled.

Then he swam. Like mad, faster and faster. Getting away from something that seemed able to catch him anytime it wanted.

CHAPTER XXII

Ephesus, Turkey
Seven Years After Event

Lincoln Pierce wore sunglasses, a long coat and a wide brimmed hat as he stepped across the barren field, past the overturned stones, and over the cracked earth. The small patch of wild grass grew there near the broken columns, the thin blades singed at the tips. He reached into his pouch, pulled the canteen, and splashed water over it and then spruced the few tufts of grass as best he could.

He'd lose this fight, he knew. This little stand of grass would eventually die, like all the other grasses. Eventually it would be all the plants, all the trees, and then he wondered if he would suffocate first or starve.

The earth was dying. He had his theories on why.

Whatever crossed seven years ago, whatever broke free, broke the earth. Shattered it somehow. Split the core.

The iron core, he figured, perhaps was no longer rotating and as consequence the magnetic field around the earth was failing.

That's why the birds were falling from the sky. They were exhausted from flying because their migrations were screwed up. They could no longer 'see' the magnetic field. That's why the satellites were dropping. The magnetic field, their insulator, was weakened and charged particles from space were frying their circuits.

It's why the aurora had been visible, even in the day. The sun's rays were bouncing off the atmosphere, but the magnetic field had been reduced, so the sun was cooking the Earth.

That's why it had gotten so hot.

Because they were burning to death.

Ironic, he thought. That hell had first come with a freeze, but it would be the fire that claimed them after all.

Lincoln didn't know how long the earth had left. How long he had left. Perhaps that's why lately he'd been thinking more about his father.

About why they had stopped talking.

After Father Zula had tried to molest him as a boy at school, his father had lost his job as a janitor and was arrested for attacking the priest. It took his mother two weeks to scrounge up enough money to bail him out. His father just sat there in jail, waiting, because they were poor.

When he did get home, things went from bad to worse. His father couldn't find work. He started drinking again, and then one night, he and Lincoln's mother got into a fight about money. His father stormed out of the house, and Lincoln remembered hearing the rev of the truck as it peeled out of the driveway.

The next morning, Lincoln went to get his bike and saw something strange. His dad's pickup was missing the PVC pipe on top of the roof rack. Lincoln thought that was strange because he'd never seen the truck without the pipe on it. He thought at first someone stole it, and then wondered if his dad got a job.

Later that evening, the police showed up at the front door. Witnesses said they'd seen a white truck swerving down the interstate the night before and it veered into the lane of a minivan. The van ran off the road and flipped six times.

Turns out there was a family in that minivan. Three kids. Two adults. All of them killed.

They weren't wearing their seatbelts and in Lincoln's imagination, the bodies were scattered like seed across the highway.

His father's truck just kept going. He was probably too drunk to even realize what he'd done.

His father wept as he was arrested. Sobbed like a baby.

Lincoln was so angry. So angry that his father could betray them like that. By the end of his senior year, he'd lost his dad. There wasn't much of a trial and his father spent three years in prison. In that time, Lincoln went off to college. *He* made something of his life. And when he did go home with Carol Connors on his arm, it was only to rub it in his father's face.

See? See what I became?

He was so angry.

Angry that his father wasn't there for him. That his father's actions had cost his family everything.

That night, the night of Carol Connors, Lincoln and his father got into a fight. Not because he was a janitor. But because he was a criminal who would only ever be a janitor.

Lincoln fluffed the dying grass and re-packed the canteen in his pouch. As he stood, he heard something in the tree line. He scanned the dead trees, and even with his sunglasses and hat, he still had to shield his eyes from the burning sun. The tree leaves had long since dropped, all that was left were whitewashed trunks.

He didn't see anyone there, but he still heard footsteps among the fallen branches.

He adjusted his bag and debated about whether to explore the sound further or to turn the other direction. He decided on the latter, because his rifle was back at the house, and he cursed himself for leaving it there because he hadn't seen another person in years.

He turned as casually as he could, but as he did, he heard the person following him in the tree line.

"Who's there?" he called.

Then he saw.

She emerged from the trees as if she'd been waiting there all along.

She was as he remembered her when he first saw her in the church. Before the key had taken its toll.

She moved toward him, and he knew she couldn't be there, because he had buried her in a tomb of concrete, and he had just watered her gravesite.

Seven years. It's been seven years.

He found himself moving toward her ghost, and then his mind was gripped by the reminder of the thing he had seen during the hell winter. When he had thought for sure it was his father talking to him in that secondhand store and instead it was just those things using his father as bait.

It's me.

He heard the voice in his head. Her voice. Clear as could be.

She moved toward him, and she was standing there, close enough to touch. He couldn't resist. He didn't care if she was powered by some dark force because he was so tired of being alone.

He reached out. Yes! She was there somehow. She held his hand. He felt her fingers on his skin. Her touch was real and if she wasn't, he didn't care. He'd take it anyway. Then she spoke again.

It's time.

* * *

He did as she told him to do. He dug up the grass that he'd tried to preserve all these years, and then went deeper into the ground. The heat was blistering, and with every shovel full of earth, the heat weighed on him even more.

It took him hours to get to where the shovel scraped the concrete box. He traced around it with the edge of the shovel, and then climbed back out of the pit. He took a swig from his water jug, then paused and stared toward the forest. He feared he was being watched and the one who she had told him was coming, had come early. He grabbed the hammer and chisel and went back down into the pit.

He chiseled her out, piece at a time, until he could make out little tuffs of the white webbing that had mixed with the concrete. He kept going, little baby strikes so he didn't injure her, until he could make out her silhouette. When he saw her, he was stunned. The white webbing had continued to grow into the concrete, and she was encased in roots and the flaky, white cocoon. He wondered if she had woken over and over all these years, only to suffocate again and again, or if the cocoon had kept her in some kind of hibernated state.

When she was free of the concrete tomb, he dragged her to the surface. He pulled her out, gently, and then lifted her over his shoulder and carried her to the remnants of a stone wall of the old church.

He laid her down gently and looked at her, and wanted to touch her hair, her skin. All he could see though was the spindled webs that cocooned her body, and he couldn't make out a face beneath. Perhaps she didn't even have one.

He could change the plan, he thought. Take her with him. Be together one last time. But he didn't. He stuck with what she said to do.

He looked to the key in her hands. He could take it. Open the book right now. See what it knew. Perhaps Lincoln's story was in there, and the book had already written what was coming. Then he'd know if they made it. But he didn't do that either.

He looked at the Mercedes parked just down the hill, and then back to the tree line.

Son of a bitch is out there, somewhere.

Lincoln touched her cocoon, one last time, and then trekked down the hill. He gave her one last look before he climbed in the car, released the brake, and a few minutes later he was speeding down the highway. He went over the list again in his mind. He had enough spare gas tanks in the trunk to get him where he needed to go. He had three spare tires, because he wasn't sure how rough the roads would be. Then he double checked the backseat. Nestled on the cushion, sat the book.

He had traced the route on the map a million times before this ride, and when he got on the 320, he knew where he was going. Abandoned cars still clogged the main highway, so he had to weave in and out, and when it got too backed up, he drove on the median. Other than the scattering of broken-down vehicles, and skeletons scattered across the highway, it was just like old times. He even turned on the radio, but there was nothing but silence.

So, he decided to hum.

CHAPTER XXIII

Ephesus, Turkey
Seven Years After Event

Longinus navigated the horse through the ruins of the church. He adjusted his hat to shield himself from the incessant sun, and then rode into what was once the main sanctuary.

He had tried to remember if he had been to this place before, but his mind was too far adrift. He was losing the ability to tell the real from the imagined. All of his storylines bled into each other, and he couldn't decipher the now from the then.

When he saw her there, laid out on the remnants of a church wall, he wasn't sure if he was dreaming again. He dismounted, and walked over, and stared down at the girl wrapped in the cocoon of the Christ. She been placed here like she'd been waiting for him all along. He scanned the surroundings, looking for someone who might jump out and ambush him. He saw no one.

Beneath the white webbing, he could see that she still clutched the key. He lifted her, gently, and carried her over to the horse. He laid her over the saddle and led the horse down to the docks where he found a decent boat. He loaded her into it and placed her gently in the cabin below.

Soon, he was on the sea again. Sailing toward Patmos.

CHAPTER XXIV

Somewhere in the Aegean Sea
Seven Years After Event

When he made it to the first island, Sunday collapsed just past the wave break. He fell in the sand, the grit all over his face and mouth, and he was too tired to care. The inner drill sergeant, perhaps it was even his father's screaming voice, roused him and he was on his feet again, wandering deliriously toward the docks.

Once there, he saw the boats, and he took one and began the journey to Patmos. He readied the sails, and the canvas thankfully filled with hot wind, and he was making decent time.

Still he was miles out, and he had not heard her whisper to him again, and he feared he was too late.

When he arrived off the coast, he thought to return to the docks, but because of the vision he'd seen of the fisherman standing over Mara and Kat, he decided against it. Instead he navigated around the far side of the island, and ran the boat aground, and jumped into the surf and waded ashore.

Sunday raced up the hill, and squinted in the sun, and in the distance, he saw a billow of dark smoke near the island's monastery.

He stuck to the hillside, and side roads so he wouldn't be seen, and as he ran the heat scorched his lungs. He avoided as much of the town as he could, until he had no choice, and he moved through the white-washed village, toward his home.

Once there, he saw the door wide open and his gut sank.

He approached slowly, wondering if he needed the guns he'd collected and hidden in the cave, but he couldn't wait. He had to know.

The table was flipped over inside the house. He checked the bedroom, and the back of the house, but they weren't there. In the corner though, he found the dog. He kneeled next to it, hoping Carrots was just sleeping, but knowing he was not.

He reached out, and slowly pet the dog, and he could feel its skull beneath its thin skin. But it had not starved. It was caked in blood and had been beaten to death.

There was a rev inside of him. The engine of old. They had come into his home and taken the things most sacred to him.

And he would kill them all.

He grabbed his binoculars and a pair of boots and moved up the hill toward the cave. He stuck to the trees instead of the roads, until he reached the church sanctuary built around the cave. Those among the village who still came here to pray, were devout enough not to disturb any of the artifacts. Once inside the cave, he stepped toward a large painting and shifted it aside, and there he saw the crate as he had left it.

He pried open the box and there was the rifle and gear.

He pulled out the M4 and checked the load. He strapped on the bulletproof vest and loaded the spare mags into the pockets.

As he did, he paused and looked to the painting that had hid the weapons. It was of Christ, with John the Apostle resting on a stone below looking up toward the heavens. This was the cave where Christ had given John his Revelation. In the painting Christ emerged from a clouded ring of fire, and at his feet were the winged heads of angels or demons, and He held two keys.

Sunday clutched the rifle as he stared at the painting. He peered into the eyes of the Son of God, expecting perhaps some epiphany, but all he saw was dirty paint stained by years of candle soot.

Once outside, he climbed the roof of the sanctuary that housed the cave and scanned the sun-bleached valley below. The villagers had massed near the docks a half mile away. It appeared the whole village was down there, some seventy strong, but He didn't see Kat or Mara among them.

They stared out across the water though, and he too searched the sea. In the distance there was a pale sail on the horizon. The incoming vessel eventually neared and docked and he watched as a man stepped off the boat.

A moment later some of the villagers boarded the boat, went into the cabin, and then returned to the deck carrying what looked like a long, rolled-up white blanket. Instead, he saw it was more bundled, like a cocoon, and he realized then that it was the body of Tom Ferguson's daughter, Eve.

The crowd moved toward the monastery, carrying the body, and it was there he saw a pillar of black smoke billowing in the sky.

He snuck down the hill, through what he hoped was the empty village, toward the monastery. He climbed the backstairs to the third-floor balcony and made his way so he could peer over the wall and into the courtyard below. It was there a huge bonfire had been built in the center of the square and the smoke hid him well.

The villagers gathered in the courtyard, and he half-expected the men carrying the cocoon corpse to toss the woman onto the flames, but instead they carried her into the chapel. The rest of the crowd though stopped and looked up. Toward him. And then he realized they weren't staring at him, but behind him, just over his head. He turned and he saw.

On the stone archway of the dual bell tower.

There they were.

His gut seized, and then he felt a pain in his heart, and he doubled over, and slid down against the wall as he looked up at them. They had been crucified. Their bodies spread out upon the stone, the nails driven into a wooden post, her feet so small, Kat's hair draped over her face. A bell hanging over each of their heads, their bodies stiff.

Sunday cried, a silent choking cry, and spoke to a being that only seemed to live in his head.

God...

Please.

It was a plea to finally come down and intervene. To show Himself. To right the wrongs.

He looked back up, through tear-stained eyes to face them, to see them once more.

And he felt the heat from the fire below, but this one burned from the inside.

CHAPTER XXV

Patmos, Greece
Seven Years After Event

Longinus sat in the pew at the front of the small church. Across from him, the child sat sprawled across the bishop's chair, lounging and kicking his little feet.

Eve suddenly seized on the altar. Her body twitched and shifted, like a spasm, and then she sat straight up. She was still covered in the web, and beneath it, her mouth opened and closed like a fish.

The candles flickered and Longinus felt the chapel grow cold, and he watched as the white web around her filled with inky black, and he knew there was something else in the church with them. He felt it emerge with her waking. He still could make out no face beneath her webbing, her body black, and as her dark mouth opened, she let out a long exhale, and with that the church filled with rank.

The boy dutifully hopped off the chair and moved toward the webbed woman on the altar. He kneeled in front of her as she convulsed, her open mouth filling the air with her stench. With each seized breath, Longinus knew it was here again in the land of men.

The church walls shuddered, and from the woman poured the feculence, and it clouded the room as the kneeling child breathed it in.

There was one final, seized breath and then Eve collapsed on the altar, and the boy stood slowly and turned, his eyes closed. When he opened them, he looked to Longinus.

And he heard the voice clearly. The voice he had not heard inside him for so many years. The voice that peeled away all things. When it spoke, all that was left was the hollow, as if he were some plastic shell, only to be made alive and real by the will of this thing.

With that, he was suddenly on his knees. Bowing. Bowing before the child in the throne because this child was the dark of the universe. And he knew. Knew what was coming. That in the end, there would be nothing left but the One.

* * *

Outside the church, John Sunday resorted to what he knew best. To kill. Fuck forgiveness. Fuck God.

In the shadow of his dead wife and daughter, he took a knee behind the half wall of the third-floor balcony as a few members of the congregation began to move up the stairs. They were coming.

He heard a whisper.

Daddy. Don't.

He looked to his dead daughter, but she only hung there mute and cold, and he pulled the rifle to his shoulder.

He knew now what the fire in the courtyard was for. They were coming up to retrieve the bodies. To pull them down from their stone perches and burn them. Burn them with hopes that if Mara had the ability to come back, like Eve did, the fire would take away that power. Leave her nothing but bone.

They. Will. Not. Take. Them.

He came over the edge of the balcony with the rifle and felt the squeeze of the trigger like an old friend, and reigned down rounds upon those coming up the stairs. Upon the crowd. He chewed them up with succinct bursts, the courtyard filled with their screams, and he quickly replaced the mag and popped in anew.

And he yelled as he did it, as he felt each round as it burrowed into their bodies, and it felt good. It felt good to kill. And he would do so it until it was done.

* * *

Eve woke.

She immediately sat up as if she'd been pulled. Her eyes opened, but she saw only milky white clouds, and she brought her hand to her face and wiped and cleared the molt from her face.

It's happened.

With her eyes still blurry, she tried looking again. She was in some…church? There were candles burning. She looked down and…

The key.

Yes, still there in her hand.

She was thirsty. In her near blindness, she could make out a silhouette. There, someone small sitting in the corner.

She heard the voice in her head. The dark whisper.

Free us.

She tried to wipe more of the blur from her eyes, but she did not need to see, to know.

They left you the key because they can't use it. Can't wield it.

"You know I will not," she said.

This world dies. With it, so shall you. And there will be no more.

"What you say is true. For both of us."

Use the key. Open the gate. Let us find a new place.

"Wherever you go, you will corrupt."

As will you.

"Ever since the bite of the serpent, you have sowed your seed within us. Turned our Eden into a pit."

I gave you what you were not supposed to have.

She turned, her vision returned, and she could see the boy reclining in a bishop's chair.

"You filled us with your filth."

We gave you the key! To all things. And now you won't even open the door for us. If you will not use it to free us, then…free him.

Eve turned and saw a man standing in the front row. Lincoln's face and body were connected and smeared into an older black man, perhaps his father. They were strung and stretched together like some kind of human amoeba.

"Lincoln?"

He tried to speak to her, but no sound came out, and his twisted, smeared eyes wept.

He was a broken man worn by hell.

Use the key. End this.

Eve slowly shook her head. She would not. She could not.

There is another.

With that, another creature stepped out of the shadows of the church. He clicked on bone spurred hooves as he moved toward the altar. She recognized his face, although smeared and congealed so that it mixed with the other faces of its hide.

"Daddy?"

He tried to speak to her as well, but his voice made no sound.

No. It's a lie. It's all a lie.

The boy hopped off the throne and stepped toward her.

It does not have to be this way. You know where they both go in the end. You know no matter what happens, they will only ever come back. To me.

But I too can build heavens. Look:

With that, Eve's eyes filled with a vision. She stood on the deck of a sailboat, the sun setting a red glow across the sea and she felt the wind in her hair. The salty air was on her tongue and the smell of the sea in her nose as she looked down and realized she held a baby. A baby she knew was hers.

Lincoln was at the helm and he smiled at her. She knew, somehow, they had made a life together and this was the world where they could be together and sail away.

She picked up the baby and brought it over to a chair on the deck of the boat, and there, beneath a wide brimmed hat, her father had fallen asleep. She sat next to him, and he woke and smiled, and reached out and he held the baby, and he was happy. Genuinely happy.

She felt the cool breeze and the joy in her heart and…

End this. End their suffering. End all our suffering.

She turned and looked out across the water for the source of the voice that was speaking to her. When she turned back, they had disappeared, and she was alone on the boat.

It's not real.

"I cannot."

Then know hell.

She suddenly stood on the edge of a dark swirling abyss, and stared into its eternal darkness, and felt her body being pulled. She screamed as she was stretched and ripped apart. Her flesh was being pulled into the pit. Every cell of her body, every atom, being peeled out of her. She would become…nothing.

But he will not get the key—

YOU will never get the key.

Her skin was peeling off her. The fire from this cosmic abyss sizzled and bubbled her flesh. She was melting, but somehow still alive, aware, even though her skin boiled, and her flesh and veins were ripped from her by the hell winds.

She tried to scream, but she had no instrument left to make a sound, and instead she could only think:

God! Please!

Suddenly there was something…

Something beyond the sound of her own scream-ing in her mind—and she felt nothing—no pain, but heard…

What? What is it?

Gunshots.

And then she knew that she still clutched the key and she was back in the church. Lincoln and her father were gone.

The church doors opened and there, at the end of the aisle, carrying a rifle, stood the one-eyed man.

* * *

Sunday stepped through the doors, rifle ready, the bar-rel hungry. He saw a man there near the altar. The boy Jacob next to him.

Sunday pulled the trigger to shoot them both down, but as he did, there was no shot. Instead the round rolled out of the front of the barrel and clinked on the ground. The rifle sagged in his grip, and turned to black putty in his hands, as if he were holding melting wax.

He heard a voice then in his head. His body was no longer his to control. He was paralyzed again, back in a coma.

I am the All. The Only.

The man standing next to the boy was coming down the aisle toward him, and he pulled a sword from a sheath on his belt. Sunday tried to move but couldn't. Instead he was suddenly forced to his knees.

His body was being controlled by someone—something—else.

He looked up at the man with the sword. His face was covered in scars.

Belac?

"Call me Longinus," he said as he pointed the sword inches from Sunday's throat. The boy came up next to him and smiled. He spoke, but his lips didn't move.

Do you think you can stop this? There is no salvation. See.

Sunday's eyes opened wide, and he was standing on a dirt road, the sky above tangled with roots that somehow grew in the clouds. There were rows of crucifixes along the path and nailed to one, her skin flailing like a sail in the wind, was the remnants of Kat. On the surrounding crucifixes was her father, and the priest, and the junkie, and the boy in the blue winter coat. All of them were still alive, and they squirmed on the long road, their flesh peeled and flayed in sheets.

The child stood next to Sunday on the road. The child looked up and smiled, proud of his work.

This is where she has always been. You have been, and always shall be—mine.

The child pointed.

Sunday looked up and there, nailed on a cross next to her, was himself.

You have spent an eternity together. Dreaming of something more together.

Sunday's gut sank. Somehow this echoed as truth. That he'd only ever belonged to the beast.

You exist because I allow you. I am your maker.

Sunday stared at the child, and he knew then, he had no power. No gun. No hope. His place on this earth was but illusion, and at night, when the nightmares came and the shadows moved, it was the creatures there to remind him that he was theirs all along, and they were watching. Watching his little pretend life-show, masturbating to him and to it, because he was a dream, they themselves could not conjure.

See.

He was back on his knees on the church floor, and he looked up at the child and saw the child's face was deep and dark, and inside it were a billion galaxies and stars, and Sunday knew then his entire universe only existed inside this thing. That as far as he could see, as far as anyone could ever see, all of existence and hope was only ever inside this thing's head. And he owned all the lands. And all the real estate.

Sunday crumbled inside, and he wanted to bow over and over, to worship this thing because he felt so, so small. He wanted to beg it for forgiveness and mercy because it could toy with him, destroy him, abuse him any way it wanted, and then do it all over again. He was a garden bug being rolled between cosmic fingers.

The boy moved toward him, his dark mask of a face moving closer. Sunday screamed, but no sound came out because he had no voice.

The man grabbed hold of the back of Sunday's head to steady it as he began to press the tip of the sword into his throat.

"Say hello to the boat-keeper," the centurion said.

"ENOUGH!" a voice boomed.

A bright white light flashed from the front of the church.

When Sunday's eyes adjusted, he saw the woman, Eve, stood near the altar, beneath a wooden cross. Her hand radiated like she held the sun. She moved down the aisle toward him as Longinus and the child stepped away from her.

"Back!" she shouted.

They did as she said, and they seemed afraid, and she reached down, and Sunday felt her hand on his arm. She lifted the key and slammed it down hard on the wooden pew, and Sunday's eyes wobbled in his skull, and the church fell apart before him like petals falling off a rose.

The centurion and the boy next to him shifted to red, and then they were very, very far away, and Sunday followed the woman Eve as she reached out and held his hand, and they stepped together through the darkness.

As she spoke, her voice drifted like it was a thousand miles away.

"Close. Your. Eyes."

He did as she said, and a second later, there was a blinding white flash, so bright he could see it beyond his closed eyelids, and when it was dark again, he opened them.

He stood then, back in a cave. As his vision returned, he saw it was the cave where he had kept the guns. The cave with the Jesus painting.

The Cave of the Apocalypse.

CHAPTER XXVI

Athens, Greece
69 CE

The market street was busy. Cornelius followed from a distance and kept up with the man in the crowd. The man who had once been named Longinus.

Cornelius watched as Longinus stopped and shopped for figs, as he did every morning. He had trailed him now for a month, following his routine. Learned his ways. Many years had passed since they'd met on the street in Brindisi. Since the attack that had killed the soldier and his wife in Italy they had both changed, but Cornelius was the only one who seemed to be growing older.

Cornelius moved to a corner, where he could watch Longinus rummage through a pouch he always carried. He had long wondered what else was in that pouch. As he sifted through it, Cornelius saw he pulled out a coin and paid for the fruit and moved on through the market.

He followed him again, knowing he would eventually eat the figs while sitting on Lycabettus Hill. He never stopped to visit any temples or altars on his morning journey. He never sought out any followers of the way. He was a solitary man of means, who, according to the shopkeepers in the market, had lived in Greece for several years. He kept some Roman ways, because of the gladius he still kept on his hip.

Cornelius had studied him for some time. Even before he trailed him through the market streets, he had seen Longinus through the visions of Peter. When they had traveled together, he'd once been close to Peter as he held the key and had a vision. Peter reached out and touched him, and when he did, Cornelius was back in the memory.

He was again standing in the atrium of Longinus' home where the centurion's body was wrapped in a white cocoon on the floor, his dead wife lying in a pool of blood next to him. As he stood there, back in this wretched time and place, he watched the dead centurion rise again and scream as he dropped to his knees and held his dead wife in his arms, rocking her back and forth. Then Longinus stood and walked toward Cornelius, his face melting and changing, a new face every time.

"See what you did?" the centurion said as he stared right at him.

When the vision was over, Cornelius spent some time trying to figure out how this man could return from the dead. The white cocoon he'd seen in the vision was some clue. Peter had told him that when he first entered the tomb after the resurrection, he had seen the remnants of what looked like white spindled silk on the slab where the Lord had rested. When he saw the Lord later, His face had changed and the others did not recognize him.

When Cornelius spoke to Lazarus about his own resurrection, he had hoped it would offer more clarity. That perhaps he too had the same ability. Lazarus said that he looked the same before and after his death.

Instead Lazarus told him the Lord had come to him inside the tomb, and he was woken by a bright light, and when he suddenly sat up; his Lord was sitting next to him, with the light glowing in his hand.

Lazarus said he looked down at his grave linens, and asked, "Did I die?"

"You were merely sleeping," the Lord told him. "And they have buried you. Now wake and leave this dark prison."

And when Lazarus stepped from the tomb, his Lord was somehow no longer walking behind him, but instead was waiting for him outside of the cave.

A bright light.

That's what had woken him. Lazarus had been resurrected by the Lord, using the Key. Peter had told him when he held the key, he could walk through walls, step through stone. When he used it to perform miracles, it seemed to wake people somehow, change them inside, and then they could walk again. Or even raise the dead.

Yes, the key had the power to give more than just visions.

What worried Cornelius now about this process though as he followed the man through the crowd, was his age. This man was much younger than him. Longinus appeared to be in his forties. Shocking, since

Cornelius had been far younger when they'd first met. Now Cornelius was almost seventy. Too old to be chasing anyone, let alone a man thirty years younger who had already bested him with a sword even when he was in his prime.

He followed the man and saw him turn into an alley. Cornelius reached the corner of the alleyway. He hesitated, poked his head around the wall to see where Longinus had gone, and suddenly he was grabbed by his tunic and pulled into the shadows off the street.

"What do you want?! Why are you watching me?!" Longinus barked.

"I don't know what you're saying sir," Cornelius said. "I'm just here to shop."

"Nay, you follow me! Why?"

Cornelius sighed. Perhaps he could reason with him.

"Because I have been sent by the followers of the way. To retrieve the key that you carry in your pouch."

"My key?"

"The one that opens the doors to other worlds. The one that shows you visions of things to come."

Longinus studied Cornelius' face, and then pushed him away and shoved him farther down the alleyway.

"Your mind has failed you, old man," Longinus said as he turned.

Cornelius was scared. He was no match for this man. He pulled his sword, his hands trembling. Longinus slowly placed his hand on his own sword.

"The key. Give it to me," Cornelius said, trying to sound tough, but he was already out of breath from panic.

"Now," Longinus said as he drew his sword, "you are finally being honest. You're here to rob me."

Longinus swung the blade toward Cornelius who raised his sword and blocked the strike easy enough, and Longinus swung back through again. Cornelius stepped back as Longinus struck wide, and Cornelius saw a momentary opening. He jabbed the blade quickly into Longinus' side and felt the blade pierce and the centurion gasp on the other end of it.

He had done it. He had bested him! In his mind, Cornelius had been a soldier again. And he had done it well.

But he also knew he had failed in the way.

Cornelius withdrew his sword and Longinus dropped to his knees. He knew he'd gone deep enough with the blade to tear a lung, perhaps pierce his heart.

As he watched Longinus try and hold back the blood pouring from his side, he was relieved the swordfight had ended in his favor. Because at Cornelius' age, he didn't think he had any chance of beating this man.

Longinus collapsed on the stone street, and then he felt guilt for what he had done, because even though this man could not die, he had still caused him a lifetime of pain.

Cornelius kneeled next to him and leaned in.

"I am sorry about your wife," he said.

As he said it, the dying man's eyes went wide, and Longinus stared up at him.

Cornelius then yanked the leather pouch off Longinus' belt. He rummaged quickly through it, and saw…

Nothing.

There was no key.

"The key? Where is it!"

But the dead man on the street, gave no reply.

* * *

Cornelius had no choice. He watched Longinus again, this time as he was buried in a grave at the far end of town.

Three days. That's how long it had taken for the Lord to rise again. When Longinus rose again, Cornelius would be there waiting to meet him with a sword, and demand to know where the key was hidden.

Cornelius waited until the cover of darkness. He retrieved a shovel and cart, and then in the night, he dug up the dead man. Because of his years, it took him longer than it should have, and he struggled to load the corpse onto the wagon and wheeled him to a small, abandoned barn on the outskirts of the city. He dragged the man inside and bound the corpse to a chair.

Then, he waited.

On the third day, he waited anxiously, because there were no signs. The man tied to the chair had begun to rot and reek, his skin bloating, the flies drawn to his decay.

Three days after that, there was still no cocoon. No rebirth. No resurrection.

Cornelius knew then. Knew he had killed the wrong man.

CHAPTER XXVII

Patmos, Greece
Seven Years After Event

"Why are we here?" John Sunday asked.

"Because I'm too weak to take you any farther," Eve said.

He moved toward the entrance to the cave. Outside it was blistering hot. The sun radiated almost white. Below he could see the village and the monastery.

"We're not far enough. They'll find us," he said.

"As long as I have the key, they can't see us."

He moved back toward her. She was weak, and slumped against the wall, and then slid down in the corner. Her pale face was coated in what looked like concrete dust and the white remnants of the cocoon. What remained of her hair was in single strands on her head. Her eyes were gaunt and sunk in her skull.

"Tell me. What do I need to do?" he said.

She spoke, but she was hoarse, her lips chapped.

"Here," she said as she reached out. "Take it."

He looked down as she handed him an old key.

"What do I do with this?" he said.

"You must journey to save them. Bring them out."

"Who?"

"All of them," she said as she coughed.

"How do I do that?"

"The key will open the door," she said.

"To what?"

"You have woken to some of the truth. That you, the others, all of us, we are the damned. You must free them. Free their souls. Show them the way. But be warned. Where you go is another world, but it is bound to this Earth, bound to its rules. For us it is both the dream and the real. You will be flesh and bone and so you can die. If you do, you will only wake again back here to a different revelation, a different version of you in this world. But by then it will be too late."

"I don't understand what you're saying."

"The key will protect you. But its power is fading. The deeper you go, the more difficult it will be for you to use it."

Her voice turned to a whisper, and she paused to get more moisture in her mouth so she could continue.

"Cling to your love. To your belief. That there is something more. Something better. Do you believe that? That there is something beyond that loves you?"

He slowly nodded.

"Then pray to it now. Pray for forgiveness for the sins you have committed so you may wield the key," she said as she nodded toward the painting of Christ. "Only those filled with the way, can use the key and walk in its path."

He stood then, and closed his eyes, and clutched the key. It felt warm in his palm, and there was a tingling that ran up his arm and neck and into his brain. He closed his eyes, and then…

He was back on the little boat on the water. Fishing. With Mara. But he was watching this from a different perspective, as if he stood on the water next to the boat.

"What is this?" he asked.

Mara looked out at him as he stood on the water.

"The way to me is through you. This is the moment of redemption. Ask *it*."

John Sunday clutched the key, and with it, he spoke the words from his heart.

Please.

Forgive me.

Mara was somehow close to his ear and she whispered.

"I love you," she said.

He opened his eyes, and he was back in the cave and the woman was slumped in the corner.

"How am I seeing these things?" he said.

"The journey goes all ways, all times."

"If I take this, won't they find you?" he said as he looked at the key.

"Yes."

"Then I'll stay."

"No. The earth is dying. The core that protected us from the magnetic field has broken, but the core also created a field shielding us from dark energy. Energy we didn't even know existed. The planet drifted through a sea of it, trillions of particles that infected us all, turned us into terrible things. That drag pulled us out of orbit. And now we're falling. Into the sun. In three days, human life here will end. If you don't free them, then everything in our world, and theirs, will be lost. That is why they want the key. To escape."

She slumped lower against the cave wall and closed her eyes to conserve energy as she spoke.

"Listen to the key. It will whisper in your heart," she said, slumping lower to the ground. "Save as many as you can."

He nodded. He thought to say something, to ask something more, but she was already fading.

Instead, he raised the key above his head as he had seen her do and slammed it down onto a rock next to him. With that it vibrated in his hands, and his eyes went wide, and he saw things he'd never seen before.

* * *

Longinus and the boy stepped from the church and into the wretched heat. He squinted in the sun and saw the courtyard was filled with the bodies of the villagers.

He followed the child, up the winding road, toward the cave. As they climbed higher, he could see the ocean. Smell the sea air, taste the salt. The grass was dead and brown, and there were no birds in the sky, but it was one last look from high ground. One last view, before it vanished forever.

He knew what the child's presence meant. With his return to Earth, he could open the gate. Release the hell winter again. With it, there would be no more.

As they stepped into the darkness of the cave, he saw Eve lying in the corner against the rock wall.

The child kneeled in front of her. She slowly, hesitantly, looked at him. She was already near dead, spit curdled in the corners of her mouth, her face pasty white.

As she stared at the child, her eyes went wide with fear, and her pupils wobbled in her skull as the child read her thoughts. Longinus knew what that meant. He was seeing everything she'd done. Everything she'd ever known. Gauging her place. And then he would leave her stranded on some distant shore, owned and broken.

They have the book, the child said in Longinus' mind.

"Where?"

Jerusalem.

The girl screamed then on the cave floor, at whatever thought he had put in her mind, and a moment later she seized and spasmed, and tried to catch her breath like she was drowning. She was still young and when Longinus had known her before, she had been beautiful. Now, she was this wretched broken thing, convulsing on the floor, shitting herself in fear.

She, in some ways, was his daughter. A child born of his seed, like all the others. Born in his image because he had resurrected her with his own blood.

Now she died. But this time, there would be no coming back. If she did return, it would only be long enough to watch the Earth burn up and herself along with it.

He felt some pity, then. A foreign feeling. Because he knew she was going to truly die. Perhaps it was pity too for himself that his mad charade would finally cease. That he had lived long enough to see the world's end.

He also pitied her because he knew she was good. Good enough to use the key to open the gates between worlds. He had admired that because he had fallen so short of what that meant. He could never wield the key, while she did so with ease.

When she was dead, the child turned.

He's taken the key.

"Where?"

With that, Longinus felt his heart seize. He clutched his chest and groaned.

Find him.

He grabbed at the pain surging through his heart.

It—burns.

Find the key.

He collapsed on the cave floor, near Eve's feet. He was dying. He was being killed.

The child kneeled near him. Longinus heard the deafening sound of crickets. He smelled the sizzled flesh of the hell spiders, and felt the roots, and heard the clinking of the metal rail. He was returning.

Shadows moved across the cave floor. Something outside was blotting the sun.

If we can't rise, none shall.

The cave floor beneath him began to crumble away, like falling pieces of shattered glass. It opened into a tunnel, and Longinus looked down into it, and he saw the walls made of the dead.

Longinus glanced once more at the dead girl on the cave floor. What terror had the One shown her? What terror had she seen that stopped her young heart?

Nothing he hadn't seen before.

And then he fell into the abyss.

CHAPTER XXVIII

Somewhere in Turkey
Present Day

Lincoln drove down the highway, finally making what seemed like good time. He'd gotten stuck in a traffic jam of dead cars on the highway outside Konya. He couldn't pass on the median, or the bridges, and so he'd had to backtrack farther than he'd wanted. Now though, he was moving again.

His wristwatch alarm vibrated and he looked down at the arbitrary time.

She would have woken by now.

He was lost again in the thought of her. Whether she was alive. He never would have left her if she hadn't so clearly instructed him to do so. If she hadn't gone over all of it with him on the boat trip over. He wrote it all down, in his little red notebook, so even seven years later he'd remember exactly what she'd said.

But after leaving her in Ephesus, the rest of his notebook pages were blank. She hadn't been able to tell him what was going to happen after he left. Just that he needed to get the book to Jerusalem.

Whether he made it there, what happened to him, what happened to her, none of that she knew.

"All I see is black. Like it doesn't exist," she had said.

He wondered if that meant she couldn't see, because she had finally died. Or maybe the world had, and there was just nothing left to see. He knew the world was ending. He just didn't know when.

Lincoln unstrapped the watch on his wrist. He held it there a moment, looking at the time, wondering if it ever meant anything. If it was just a human construct, a meaningless attempt at order in chaos, an effort to decipher the cipher.

He took the watch and tossed it out the window.

Eventually Lincoln was driving faster, moving in between still cars, and back to the median when he suddenly swerved.

Someone in the road!

He spun the wheel and almost crashed into a parked car, slammed the brakes, and the book in the backseat went flying onto the floorboard.

The car came to a complete stop, the engine knocked, and then it was dead again.

Lincoln grabbed a .38 from the glovebox and jumped out of the driver's seat. He used the car as cover and pointed the gun toward where he'd seen the person in the road.

"Come out!" he shouted.

Slowly a man emerged from behind a dead car. He was Indian. Tall, bone thin, with a thick gray beard. He wore sunglasses and a dirty white kurta, and he slowly raised his hands. Lincoln could tell he was carrying something on his back.

"Please," he called out. "Don't hurt us."

"Us?!"

The Indian man slowly turned. There, strapped to his back, was an old woman, wearing a thick pair of sunglasses. She was missing her legs.

Lincoln was stunned at the sight of her little stunted body, being carried like a backpack.

He hadn't seen people in seven years. Not another living soul for so, so long.

Can I trust them?

Does it matter anymore?

"Where are you going?" he called out.

The Indian man turned back around and smiled.

"Jerusalem!"

CHAPTER XXIX

The Crossing

When his vision returned, and his brain was again able to process a recognizable reality around him, John Sunday still had no idea where he was. He had walked through a prismed distortion of light, like he'd stepped through a dark kaleidoscope and had emerged in a rock tunnel. The key in his hand radiated light, but as he stepped through the shadows, he had no idea where he was or where he was going.

He reached his hand out to guide him and felt the tunnel until he emerged into an open cave and heard scratching. As he shone the light from the key around, he saw someone wearing a cloak, their back to him, hunched in the corner of the cave.

He moved slowly toward them, wondering if they were suddenly going to spin around and attack.

He spoke so as not to startle them, but as he did, his voice sounded a thousand miles away, and it dragged like a vibrating wave around him.

Hello....

Nonetheless, they turned. Almost startled.

She was in her twenties and pretty with dark tan skin and black hair tucked beneath the hood.

What is she doing here?

He spoke again…

"Where am I?"

The words came out like a long whisper, and she either couldn't hear him, or she dismissed it, and she turned and went back to what she had been doing: scraping something into the rock. He moved behind her, close enough to see her carving what looked like a 'T.' Next to her feet was a cold, clay jar. And Sunday knew.

He was back in the cave. Back where they had first found the clay pot.

What are you doing? Who are you?

His voice drifted to his ears like molasses, and when he reached out to try and touch her, his hand slipped right through. Still, she stood and turned and looked right at him or more so, right through him.

"Mataraya," she said in a language he did not speak. But then, somehow, he still understood.

"Watcher."

With that, she turned, and she ran out of the cave toward a surface entrance, and he was about to chase her, but the light in the sky outside the mouth of the cave moved very quickly through day and night, day and night, hundreds of times in the span of seconds.

Suddenly the cave around him shook, and the entrance she had escaped from collapsed, and the rocks fell over the opening and he was again buried in the darkness.

Around the cave, there were whispers. There was a new cold in the air and a scratching sound. He shone the light toward the abyss where a long, bony hand reached over the edge and began to pull itself up. More hands, and then bodies followed, and the things scurried out of the hole toward him. They were humans, or had been, bent now and twisted like crickets as they crawled around the circle of light made by the key. Some hesitated to reach their long bone fingers out to touch the clay jar at his feet and they whispered like asps around him. They scratched and clawed at the rock wall, their fingertips just on the outskirts of the light, reaching for the clay jar, but not able to grab it.

There was more scratching, and he shone the key light, and there at the far end, was the tunnel. The narrow tunnel through which he had once crawled. The tunnel where he'd been shot in the head.

What's happening?

Why am I back here?

He watched as a light flickered around inside the tunnel, and then a person dropped out of the opening like they'd been secreted from the stone. The person scanned the cave with their light, and then he realized. It was her.

Kat.

She turned, and looked, scanning the cave with her lone light.

"Here!" he said.

She turned as if she'd heard him and scanned the headlamp back and forth across the cave. He picked up a rock and banged it on the cave wall and shouted.

She searched for the source of the sound, but moved forward, exploring the rest of the cave.

I'm reliving this. Seeing things.

The light from her headlamp fell on the clay jar, and she slowly moved toward it. As she was examining the jar, the bent human creatures crawled like bugs out of the abyss toward her. He moved the light from the key around her, pushing the creatures away from her as they scurried away to avoid the light.

"Kat! It's me!!" he said, but she couldn't hear him.

She picked up the clay jar as a sea of creatures poured from the abyss, and they crawled toward her, and now she saw them too. She panicked and flailed to check her gas sensor and started to collapse. Overcome by the gas in the cave, she fell back against the cave wall as the creatures scurried toward her.

He stood over her with the halo of light.

"Back!" he shouted. The creatures circled the light, trying to reach into it, but as they did the light burned and singed their flesh.

He heard someone else coming through the tunnel and into the cave. Then he saw himself emerge. Fit, with two eyes, and he watched himself move through the cave toward Kat. The healthier version of himself helped her with the oxygen mask, and helped bring her back, and a second later, she was back on her feet and carrying the clay pot and scurrying back to escape through the tunnel.

Sunday knew where this was going. He watched as she climbed back into the tunnel, and she disappeared. The key flickered then in his hand, and he looked at it, deciphering the light, wondering if it was just some kind of candle that could easily be extinguished.

He watched as he climbed into the tunnel to go after her and save her. He knew what happened next, and a second later, he heard a voice coming from the other end of the tunnel, and then he heard the gunshot. The one that ended with a hole in his head.

With that shot, the creatures in the darkness around him were revved. They scurried around the mouth of the tunnel, and the light he held flickered again.

He tried to use the key to ward them off, but the light was fading, and they crawled past him, and he watched as they dragged his body out of the tunnel by his ankles. He was still gushing blood from the hole in his head, still somehow kicking and screaming as they dragged him over the edge and into the abyss. With that, they were gone, and he was alone in the cave again with the dim light of the key.

He moved back to the tunnel and peered in with the light. On the other end, someone was staring back at him.

The little mute boy in the blue winter coat.

"Hey," Sunday said. "It's me!"

The boy was skittish and moved quickly from view.

"Hey! Hey!" he called into the tunnel, but the little boy had disappeared somewhere on the other side.

Sunday stared into the darkness, but the boy didn't return and so he turned back to scan the cave again, looking for some way out.

As he did, the little boy was standing there next to him.

"Christ, kid!" he said as he stumbled backward.

In the key light, the child's face still bore the gunshot wound, and half his face was concave. But his skin was also faded, almost transparent, like a child still in utero. His eyes were wide and sunken and black. The blue winter coat hung limply on him, and the bones of his fingers and his veins were clearly visible through his pale skin.

"It's me," Sunday said. "John."

The boy cowered in the corner, afraid.

"Can you hear me?" Sunday asked.

The boy nodded. He turned, slowly, hesitantly and looked toward the light.

"It's Ok," Sunday said, and he reached his hand out, gesturing for him to come forward. The little boy slowly rose, and slowly, stepped into the light.

"Why am I seeing this again? Why am I here?" Sunday said.

The boy then stood upright in the light, as if renewed by it and then he spoke, even though his lips did not move.

"You are here to bring the light of the key into the abyss," the boy said clearly in John Sunday's head. "To the one who needs it most."

The boy was speaking!

"Who? Mara? Is she here?" Sunday said.

He nodded. "She is. She preaches the way, deep in the pit. To save those from their prison. And to those that can hear her, they shall rise."

"How do I bring her the key?"

"She has shown me the way." The little boy turned and pointed toward the deep abyss in the center of the cave. The same hole from where the creatures had just disappeared and dragged his own body.

Sunday stepped toward the edge and used the light from the key to peer down into it. He saw nothing but more blackness.

Still, from deep within, he heard whispers and the faint chirping of crickets.

"Really?" Sunday said, but the boy was already starting to climb down into the pit.

Sunday hesitated and then followed, down into the last place he wanted to go.

They descended for some time over rock and tangled roots, Sunday half-expecting to be grabbed in the darkness by some clawed hand. Instead, they reached the bottom and were in another cavern. Sunday shone the light around and overhead to see from where they had climbed, but he saw no light above.

"We have to hurry," said the boy, without moving his lips. "They hunt this place."

Sunday nodded, and he and the pale mute boy emerged from the mouth of the cave. They stepped into what seemed like an outside forest, but above his head were what appeared to be dangling roots. The whole sky was made of these fibrous roots that twisted over each other and dropped from the sky and ran into the ground and became the stalks of trees. There at the base of the trees he saw bodies. They were bound to the stalks, their skin merged and melted to it so that their flesh was the bark.

A feeling of déjà vu and cold fear came over him. He was remembering pieces of this, like a dream coming back to him. With it there was a realization. He'd known battlefields. He'd known death. But this, this place was outside of his understanding. A place foreign and alien that shouldn't exist because it betrayed everything men had ever said about their pedestal in the universe.

He remembered it then as something else:

A place from which there was no escape.

They had owned him here. Fed on him, on his dreams, and...

"Hey," the boy said in his mind. "We must go."

Sunday nodded, hesitantly, his pulse throbbing in his temples and they moved quickly through the dark forest, the key their only light, until the boy suddenly heard something and stopped and tucked behind a skin root tree. Sunday followed closely behind.

Beyond the trees was the chirping of crickets, followed by the sound of something solid clicking on the rocks. Something was coming. Something was in the forest with them. He quickly took the key and hid its light beneath his bulletproof vest. He sunk lower behind the tree and looked to the cowering boy next to him, and even though the boy had closed his translucent lids, Sunday could still see his eyes. The boy had no way to hide, no way to avoid seeing what was coming for them.

Up close now, and pressed close to the tree, he saw the human mouths of the bark trying to speak to him, and he could hear the flapping of their lips.

He peered around the tree and saw a hell spider moving through the darkness. It was much bigger than the ones he had seen before. This one seemed stitched together with the bodies and bones of dozens of people. Its bone spur heels click-clicked on the rock forest floor. It was searching.

For them.

The spider scanned back and forth with the eyes from the dozens of faces in its hide, and Sunday pressed close against the tree, against the squirming mouths of the bark. He tucked lower, and the spider was there on the other side of the tree, and then it paused and looked toward the root sky.

There Sunday saw an even bigger hell spider crossing over the treetops. It defied gravity itself, a creature that on Earth could not exist, but here the ground shook as its giant bone spurs landed on the rock. As it moved overhead, he could see its belly was full of ten thousand eyes, all of them searching. He cowered, to hide from this thing that could see all, no matter how low he sunk. There was no escape and it would see them both.

The spider on the other side of the tree was moving closer, coming around the edge of the tree...

The key will protect you.

He remembered her words. He pulled it out from his vest, and dragged the mute boy closer to him, and its light shone bright in his hand, and with that the spider on the other side of the tree came around the edge of the tree to attack. Instead, it hovered there on the rim of the light and Sunday stared square into its face. Into its faces. It smelt of the decay of a hundred dead corpses, the burnt sizzle of seared flesh, the mouths and eyes moving within its hide.

The creature stared into the light. It then searched past the halo, as if it knew there was something there within, but couldn't find it. Couldn't *see* it. It moved back around the tree and then back through the forest. Overhead, the hell spider moved past as well, and with it, Sunday could again see the root sky.

He exhaled slowly and looked at the key in his hand, trying to understand what had just happened. The light that it shone, somehow, had protected them. Perhaps the light was not visible here or they couldn't see it.

And thus, perhaps, he could use it to hide.

* * *

He followed the boy as they emerged from the forest and stepped over wide, barren, ground. They passed boulders the color of flesh, and as he moved past, he saw what he thought at first were the carvings of faces in the rock. Instead he saw the rocks were the faces of people, their features twisted into each other.

The boy led, until they came to a ridge and the boy quickly ducked down to hide. Sunday followed the boy's lead and dropped to the ground, the rock cold as ice against his skin.

Somewhere beyond, there was thumping. Loud, repetitive thuds.

The boy nodded toward the ridgeline, and Sunday slowly moved over the edge and looked. From the dark root clouds, people were falling out of the sky and landed with sickening splatters onto the rocks below.

It was raining bodies.

The bodies then somehow got up again, their bones and bodies broken, their organs leaking out of them, and they dragged themselves like flesh puppets toward a bloody metal rail. On one end was a spike, about chest high, and one by one the bodies impaled themselves on the rail spike.

The rail was moving, like a giant conveyer that fed into a dark cave that looked like the half-buried head of some giant, ancient alien god.

Thousands of humans, twisted and broken and dripping, flailed on the rail line. Even in the distance, he could hear the line moving like the wheels of an ancient train car on the tracks, and despite its metal grinding he could still hear the bodies convulsing and twisting on the rail. As they lurched forward, they moaned, because somehow even in death, they *felt* their pain.

Along either side of the rail line, were towers made of huge bones. He followed the towers to their tops, and saw hundreds of huge skulls, each of their empty sockets staring down, watching over the humans being fed into the pit. Littered around their bases were more skulls, as big as elephants, as if some of the heads had long ago toppled from their sky perch and this was now a graveyard of gods.

Sunday scooted back down and looked to the boy.

"Is that the only way in?" he asked.

The boy nodded, and he was breathing fast, and it was obvious now to Sunday that the little dead boy was just as scared as he was.

Sunday looked to the key in his hand.

"Will they see us?" he asked.

The pale mute boy shrugged.

Sunday took a breath.

He remembered again this place. Remembered it not as some obsolete, but as an absolute. Remembered it as it was: an alien world beneath the feet of men, invisible to the living, visible to the dead.

And he was afraid.

He reached out for the boy's hand, partly to be there for the boy, partly to know that he was not alone. And the pale mute boy gave it to him.

Under the halo of the fading key light, they moved over the ridge. He expected to be picked off right then and there by some hell spider waiting to ambush. Perhaps by some giant bone hand that came from the sky and scooped him from existence. Instead, they moved into the trench, the rail line of bodies moving over their heads, and he saw them better: impaled through their spines, their bodies writhing like flapping flesh sails.

One caught his attention on the line: a small, naked older lady who stared down at him. She was wearing pasty white make-up and her gray hair had been done up like she'd just come from church, and she watched him until she drifted past. He knew she was aware. She may have been dead, but that word had no meaning here.

Sunday looked past the line, toward the skeleton skyscraper towers overhead, their giant bone heads swaying, almost nodding, as they creaked in the winds. He clutched the key tightly, and held the boy's hand just as tight, as they stepped into the mouth of the cave. Beyond it, he saw nothing but darkness.

CHAPTER XXX

Somewhere in Turkey
Seven Years After Event

Lincoln drove, the Indian man in the front seat, the crippled old woman propped up in the backseat. The sun was noticeably bigger in the sky.

He looked over at the man, who despite the pending end of the world, smiled like an idiot. Lincoln wondered if he was crazy. If he kept a knife hidden somewhere beneath that dirty kurta, and would stab Lincoln to death, steal the book and perhaps most importantly, his new car.

The Indian man looked over at him and continued to grin. "I am Dharmapuri Thirumala Venkata Manoj Anantharam." He smiled even wider, as if he knew what question was coming next. "Call me Dharma. And this…"

He turned to introduce the woman in the backseat, and Lincoln prepped for another mouthful of vowels.

"…is Mother," the Indian man said.

Lincoln glanced in the back and nodded to the legless woman propped there, held upright by her seatbelt, like he was driving around the top half of a mannequin.

"Why are you going to Jerusalem?" Lincoln asked.

"Same reason as you," he said.

"Well, man, I don't honestly know why I'm going there."

Dharma smiled even bigger. "Same!"

Lincoln looked over at him trying to figure out whether this guy was a loon. He nodded toward the backseat. "How long have you two been on the road?"

"Since Germany."

"You walked from Germany?"

The Indian nodded again.

"Why?" Lincoln asked. "I don't get it. What happens in Jerusalem?"

"I don't know."

"So, you just set off one day to walk three-thousand miles from Germany to Israel because you felt like it?"

"No. Because of the song."

"Song?"

"The one we heard," Dharma said as he looked to his mother and smiled. "You haven't heard it?"

Lincoln shook his head.

The Indian looked in the backseat again and spoke to his mother in Hindi. She nodded. Dharma turned back around.

"After the winter, we were starving. It was just the two of us. Mother was dying, and she told me when she died, I was to eat her."

Lincoln looked over at him.

"I told her when this happened, I would follow. For without her, there was no reason to live. That I would not take what little was left of her. And then, something strange happened. Our bellies were round and fat."

"From hunger?"

"No. The hunger was *gone*. We settled back in together, fat and full, and as we did, we both saw a blinding white light. And from within, we heard a song. It came into both our hearts, like someone had plucked a string inside us. And we longed to hear that song again. To feel it inside because it had *fed* us. The song did not speak, but in our minds, we both knew what we had to do. So, we rose, and we began the journey. Bound for the golden dome we see in our dreams."

"What dome?"

"The one in Jerusalem," Dharma said.

"The Dome of the Rock?" *Is that where I'm supposed to go?* "But you're Hindu, right?"

"Yes."

"And you're headed toward a Muslim shrine?"

"It is where we will wait for the truth."

"Whose truth? Yours? Mine? Theirs?" Lincoln asked.

"Truth is one. But it has many names."

"What happens there?"

"We wait for the coming of Kali and Kalki. They will close the curtain of time."

The Indian man just smiled. Lincoln turned and looked again at the woman in the back seat. She had an even bigger smile on her face.

"Look," Lincoln said. "You seem to know a lot more about this than I do. I was just told to drive the book to Jerusalem. Do you know what's in the book?"

"It goes by many names. The Book of Life. The Book of Names. But it is the final revelation."

"Of what?"

"Of us. Of our individual deeds. The book is one, but it is each of us and how we shall be judged. As individuals and as a species."

"That book contains everything every human has ever done. Must be really small print."

"We are all written in the book," Dharma said. "Before we were born, while we are here, whether we return."

"What happens when the book is opened?"

"Like all books, it will be read. But Kali will try and stop that from happening so that no human shall cross into the new age. What you carry my friend, is not a book. It is a *ticket*."

Lincoln didn't ask any more questions. Instead, he just drove on in silence and stared out at the open road ahead. He didn't know how he felt about dying or how he felt about being judged by some cosmic deity. That had been such a foreign concept to him for much of his life. Now, here it was, for real. If what this crazy Indian was saying was true, in a matter of hours he would stand face to face with some cosmic maker and be weighed by a being that was apparently infinite and vast and—judgmental.

Was he worthy of a heaven?

Was it too late to repent? Or go to church? What golden ticket did he have to punch? Did he need to do some noble deed in the last hours to redeem a life that wasn't necessarily sinful, but one that had been—selfish? He hadn't really done anything to help anyone in his life, other than himself. He hadn't donated to charities, or volunteered to help feed the homeless, or even gotten a puppy from the pound.

He glanced back at the book on the backseat and wondered what it had to say about him. The crippled old woman rested her fingers on it and tapped them like she was anxiously waiting to open it.

Eventually, they hit an open stretch of highway with fewer cars. As Lincoln contemplated what the Indian had said, he noticed the sunlight that had been beating down on him was beginning to fade. Dark clouds, black as ink, passed in front of the sun, and for the first time in years, Lincoln thought it might rain.

He looked farther down the highway. Sure enough, it looked like they were driving into a storm. But as they neared, the outside air turned very cold, and instead of rain, he saw what fell on the windshield.

Snow.

CHAPTER XXXI

John Sunday and the child were going deeper in the cave, and the temperature was getting colder. The flesh on the line overhead reeked and their entrails and fluids dripped on them as they moved into the depths.

They emerged into a giant cavern and there underground was a vast, dark shore. They were far below the surface, on the edge of some sprawling black lake, and in the light of the key, he saw the rail line extended over the water like a viaduct and disappeared into the dark distance of what seemed an eternal cave.

Sunday stood on the edge, the sludge lapping the shore, wondering how they would cross. There was no way he was going to swim that filth.

"What do we do?" he asked the boy.

"Wait."

"For what?"

"The boats-man."

As they sat on the shoreline, the sound of the bodies moving on the line overhead, Sunday couldn't help but stare at the boy as he sat there playing with rocks. He was still the boy that he had known before, even though he was near translucent.

"That was you. Before? In the cave, talking to me when I was shot?" Sunday said.

The boy nodded.

"And you were there at the construction site, the day I tried to kill myself. And when I was being tortured?"

The boy nodded again.

"How is that possible?" Sunday asked.

"This place has no clock. What happened a million years ago, a thousand years ago, is also now."

Sunday looked to the line above as the moving bodies disappeared into the darkness.

"How are you here, while they're..."

"Mara freed me. Because of it, I am a shade of both worlds, and she released me to guide you to her. And she allowed me to see what this place really is."

"What's that?"

"A prison. But one you can't see."

"You couldn't see this was a prison?" Sunday asked as he pointed to the bodies moving overhead.

The boy shook his head. He seemed saddened by it. "No."

With that, a pale light emerged on the water from the mouth of a far cave.

The boy stood, panicked.

"We have to hide!" he said, his lips still not moving.

Sunday stood and watched as a flat barge moved through the darkness, and as it neared, he could hear oars in the water. He turned and he and the boy ran and hid behind a large rock near the shore.

"Hide the key!" the boy spoke still only in Sunday's head, but nonetheless he whispered. "Charon sees all!"

Sunday tucked the key into the pouch of his bullet-proof vest. From behind the rock, Sunday watched as the boat neared and beneath the pale dangling light of the lone candle on board, he saw a haggard old man in a tattered brown cloak on the barge.

The barge slowed and drifted toward something Sunday couldn't see in the water, but as the light neared it, the man onboard pulled a pole with a giant hook. He went to the edge and brought the hook down and impaled it and scooped it up and dragged it onto the boat.

Sunday could see then it was a body, one that perhaps had fallen off the rail line above and floated in the dark waters below.

The barge drifted closer to the shore and to them, and ran aground, and the man took the candle and the hook and disembarked. He hung the candle on the hook pole and as it moved closer, Sunday could see the boats-man was stitched together with various pieces and parts, but still somehow familiar. He had no eyes.

He remembered then where he had seen him.

In the back of his car. It was the homeless man who had ridden his bike past him years earlier, when he thought he was losing his mind from the coma.

He was here now and seemed very real.

Despite not having eyes, the old man scanned the dark cave. In the candlelight, Sunday saw him pause as he found the remnants of a man crawling on the ground, squirming along the rocks.

The mangled body screamed and pleaded as the boats-man neared.

The boats-man then used his giant hook and brought it down and impaled the back flesh, scooping the man up like a giant fish. The body wiggled and screamed on the hook and the old man didn't so much as groan when he lifted him.

"We have to go. Now!" said the boy in Sunday's mind.

The boy darted off, and Sunday wanted to call out to tell him to stop, but instead he paused and watched as the boy ran *toward* the barge!

What's he doing?

Sunday hesitated but left the cover of the rock and raced toward the barge, his heart pounding. From somewhere in the darkness of the cave, he heard the old man impale someone else.

Together they climbed on board the barge, and there on the deck were hundreds of bodies, writhing slowly, stacked like pelts.

"We must hide!" the boy said.

Sunday looked at the boy. *Where? In the pile of bodies?*

The boy nodded, even though Sunday had not spoken.

The boats-man was returning. The boy moved into the pile of hides, and Sunday dragged a body over on top of the child. Then he too moved into the mound and dragged a body on top of him. It was a man, around forty. His lips had been stitched shut, and there appeared to be some kind of plastic wedged in his eyelids. Beneath the lids, it appeared his eyes had dried and shriveled like raisins. Tufts of cotton protruded from his nostrils. The corpse still smelled tart, like formaldehyde.

He positioned the body so he could look out and still see the deck. He watched as the boats-man boarded, and as he did, he felt the barge shift with his weight. The boats-man carried the hooked pole over its shoulder, and several bodies were impaled on the end, and he moved the pole over the mound. The bodies landed on top of Sunday, and his breath tightened as he was buried beneath more dead.

The boat set sail, and Sunday rocked back and forth beneath the weight of the bodies. They sailed for some time until the rocking ceased, and he realized they were no longer moving. He watched through a small opening as the boats-man grabbed a pile of bodies off the pile and tossed them overboard.

Sunday tried to move, to escape, but he was pinned by the weight on top of him. He was trapped.

He felt the boat lurching side to side as the boats-man disembarked and he tried to squirm free but couldn't move.

There was a kind of impaling sound, the same sickening sound he'd heard outside the entrance to the cave and Sunday realized the boats-man was sticking the bodies back on the rail line somewhere onshore. The boats-man came back on board, and reached into the pile, and plucked some more bodies off. Among them was the boy and Sunday heard him screaming in his head.

Help! Please!

Sunday struggled to bring an arm up so he could reach into his vest.

The boats-man paused and held the child up like a toy and looked at him, and he brought the child closer and stared into the child's face. The boy squirmed in the blind man's hands, and the boats-man reached for his hook-pole.

Sunday felt the key, and he pulled it out, and as he did, he was engulfed in its light beneath the pile.

Suddenly, the weight of the bodies was being relieved, and Sunday realized the boats-man was pulling them off to get to him. As the last body was lifted, he rolled from the pile and to his feet on the deck and held the key out in front of him as if it could in some way protect him.

As he did, he could see the boats-man more clearly. His eyes had been hollowed out of his head, but even blind, he looked down to the key.

"You want this?" Sunday shouted. "Come on!"

The boats-man tossed the child over the edge of the boat and pulled the hook around so he could grip it with two hands.

"The child can't save you," he hissed.

He smiled and swung the hook through the air. Sunday ducked and rolled and then jumped quickly onto the pile of bodies and the hook again landed next to him and sank into the mound. The hook stuck in the flesh and the boats-man tried to pull it back out, but as he did, the bodies seemed to cling to it and hold it down.

Sunday jumped off the boat on to the shore below, as the boats-man pried the hook free and lifted to swing again. The child was there on the ground, dazed, and Sunday picked him up and ran toward the rail line. The boats-man raced down the gangplank, with the speed of many legs beneath his tattered cloak and was closing in on them.

The spike of the rail used to impale bodies was about chest high and Sunday lifted the boy up and on top of the rail line. He pulled himself up behind him, and as they started to run down the narrow top of the rail, the boats-man slammed the hook down in front of them.

Sunday kicked square into the boats-man's face, but as he did, he felt a pull as his boot sunk into the tattered flesh. The man's skin wobbled like Sunday had only disrupted water, and he struggled to pull his foot back out. With that, the boats-man lurched his head back, and pulled Sunday off his feet. He landed hard on the rail, and now stared at him face to face.

The boats-man reached out with a long bone-thin hand and grabbed hold of the boy's ankle. The boy screamed in Sunday's mind as he was dragged over the side of the rail and landed hard on the ground.

The boats-man lifted the hook again over his head to bring it down into the boy. Sunday clutched the key, and closed his fist around it, and with that, the key illuminated.

He jumped off the rail, between the boats-man and the boy. He shot up with his fist, and punched the boats-man in the face, and this time his fist got stuck. It radiated light around the ripples of the boats-man's face.

The boats-man was engulfed in blinding light and the light shone out of his eye sockets, and a second later, the hook fell and clanked on the rock below, followed by the boats-man's smoking cloak. There was nothing left but the stench of burnt cloth.

Sunday looked at the pile of rags. The boy pushed at the rags with his foot, to make sure.

"It is also the key to Death," the boy said as he looked down.

When they had both caught their breath, Sunday and the boy climbed back on top of the rail. They ran along the top of the line until they spotted a narrow path below that threaded between the rocks. And that is the path they took.

CHAPTER XXXII

Longinus woke on the rocks, the sound of sobbing and wailing in his ears. He stood and looked at himself. He was dressed as a centurion, as if he was once again a puppet of Rome. He looked around.

He was back. Outside the cave, outside the entrance, the rail line above his head, the bodies falling from the sky. This is the place where he had come after the gate had first been opened. Until that time, death for him was merely black. But with the opening of the gate, he'd been able to cross here. To this world. To its rules.

He remembered in the cave at Caesarea Philippi, he had fallen out of life and out of this sky. He had then risen to his feet in this alien land, his body broken, and he inserted his flesh onto the metal line because that is what the voice in his head commanded him to do. He had no power to stop it, no power over his own arms and legs. It controlled everything.

Then he remembered flailing on the line as he was fed deep into the pit. Bound for the cave of frozen dreams.

He looked up at the line. This time it wasn't moving. The broken bodies were still hanging there, and they looked down at him, and they wailed and called out to him for help.

"Please," they cried.

"Please. Take us with you."

They cried for forgiveness.

"Show us the light."

The light? There is no light here.

And he knew then that the ones he sought had already been this way.

* * *

Eventually Sunday and the child came to a place where the rail line split off above their heads. It happened in a wide, open canyon where in the darkness above, in between the roots, there was a single, distant star, the only natural light they had seen so far in this place.

The rail diverged, like the branches of a tree, and as they passed some of the lines had broken down and toppled over. The bodies were still hanging there though and were withered flakes of skin flapping in the breeze. Each body though held their hollowed arms up, reaching toward the sky.

In other places, the bodies had fallen off the line and appeared to be growing out of the earth. They passed a few of those random bodies also reaching for the sky, until they found the main rail line out of the canyon and followed it until they overlooked a valley.

Sunday gasped when he saw it.

The main rail disappeared into the distance, but below it, as far as he could see, were bodies growing like corn out of the earth. The stalks were flesh, the humans encased in the pulp, and their arms meager branches that reached toward the sky.

"What...what is this place?" he asked the boy.

"The hell fields," the child said.

"What are they all doing here?"

The child pointed to the lone star. "Reaching for the light."

As they descended into the valley, they passed crops of bodies. Row after row where there were millions, perhaps billions of stalks. The faces of the people within were still recognizable. All their eyes staring skyward, their little branch arms reaching.

"This is where they wait," the boy said.

"For what?"

"For when their sins will be forgiven," the child said.

"What sins did they do to deserve this?"

"Some...perhaps none."

"None?"

"Everyone comes here," the boy answered.

"What?"

The boy gestured around him. "Since Golgotha, this, all of this, is the place where humans come. There is no other."

"No, that can't be true."

"You know it is, but you have forgotten," the child said.

"What about...Mara? What is she doing here?"

"She kneels before the abyss and prays. Prays that He forgives us for what we have done to Him. That He turns His light back toward us and saves us from what is coming."

"What's that?"

"The end. To everything."

Sunday looked again out across the field.

"No. There's more than this. I've felt it."

He looked up toward the lone, distant star. It was then he felt something strange inside himself. It was as if his mind and heart were but a single, lone string. And as he looked skyward, he felt a single faint pluck inside himself, and although he felt its vibration radiate within, it was also slowly fading. It was if that vibrating chord was his life and was him alive, and the fading was him now here. And he longed again to feel that vibration again. He looked skyward. Because it had been the source of that vibration, the source of that song within.

Then he looked down and saw the earth swallowing his feet. Even with his shoes, he felt the earth and rock and dirt burrowing into his flesh. He absorbed the earth into his body, and felt it creeping up his legs, and he tried to move, but could not.

This place was somehow connecting with him. He was becoming part of it. He was becoming the field. And then he felt them all.

Their terrible loneliness.

They had been abandoned, and they wished that He would look upon them again and play His strings inside them. That some of them were good. That they had tried to lead good lives. That they were sorry for what they had done as a species. Sorry for Eden, and the Flood, and Golgotha.

And then he saw then that this place was a prison for everyone.

The same for all.

He looked to the star.

The only light.

He was starting to fade…his mind, his memories filling with rocks.

And there were people—here—that he…

Knew.

He could no longer think. He could no longer scream.

He was claimed by the fields.

* * *

The boy moved toward Sunday and saw his face was filling with the soil. His eyes were locked skyward. The boy moved quickly, cautiously, less the earth swallow him as well.

He could see the man's face was turning into a husk, and he was changing like all the others.

He reached into Sunday's vest pocket and pulled out the key. But the key did not light up. It did not shine for him. It was just a key. He knew why. Knew that he had committed a terrible sin when he had tried to kill the baby. And the key would not work for him. Not here. Not now. Not ever.

Instead, he took the key and slid it into John Sunday's stalk fingers. He wrapped his leafy fingertips around the metal. Then he closed his little transparent eyelids and he said his prayers as his mother had taught him.

"Please," he said. But he knew that such a prayer was nothing new here. That in this field, his voice was a drop in an ocean of sorrow.

He was feeling it now. The branches and husk of John Sunday were reaching out for the boy. Clinging to him. To his flesh. And he felt the stalks enter his little body. He was going to be swallowed by it as well. He would fail and this is where they would all die. No. Not *die*. Cease to exist. Cease to ever be.

The boy raised his eyes skyward, so that he too could see the only light. The only light he'd ever known in this place. There *was* hope here. And he felt the cord inside pluck once, and it warmed him, but then it was gone. And he hoped, hoped that song would return.

He began to fade. And as the roots entered his body, he heard them. All their voices. They were weeping within, their silent plant cries and screams, audible now to his little ears. Then he saw *her*. She was here. And he so wanted to be with them again.

And then…

He saw a light.

Another light.

Something not in the sky, but below.

The key—

Illuminated.

He could see it. He could see it!

And he felt its warmth, and the song it played echoed through his little body, and he looked to John Sunday and he saw the man's eyes shift from looking skyward, down to the boy's face. And then John

Sunday looked down at the key in his hand, and the mute boy could see he knew the key had woken.

* * *

Sunday felt the key radiating through him. With it, the earth and mud and rocks and dirt fell from his face and out of his ears and mind, and he felt the beating of his own heart again.

Within the key, he heard it.

The voice he had longed to hear.

The one he sought.

And the voice said, "Daddy."

With that, he felt the blood coursing again through his flesh, and he was warm and not cold, lifeless stalk. He pulled his feet from the earth pit, and held the boy in his arms, and carried him away from the fields.

The remnants of husk on his skin burned away as the key radiated light around him. He knew then. Knew then there *was* something more to even this place. And it was love.

He was going to find them. No matter how deep he had to go. No matter where she was.

And then he said her name.

"Kat."

The key showed her to him. She was here, not in this field, but in some kind of cave. She was not *in* the cave though. She was *part* of the cave. Part of the rock. Bound to it.

He would stop at nothing to free her.

And not even God Himself could stop that.

He moved away from the field and placed the boy on the ground. As he did, the little boy looked up at him and then back across the field.

"We have to go," Sunday said.

He turned to leave, but as he did, the boy was not following him.

"What?" Sunday asked.

The child looked out at the field. Sunday followed the boy's eyes as he scanned the stalks. And then, the boy darted off, into the rows.

Sunday chased after him, calling for him as he ran, lest he be swallowed again by either the earth or something hiding in the stalks.

The boy raced through the field and Sunday did his best to keep up with him. They reached a row, much like any other, and the boy dropped to his knees in front of one of the stalks. When Sunday reached it, he saw why the boy had run.

She was here. He recognized her. She did not look like she had in the photos he had seen in the boy's house so long ago, when her face had been bright and full of life. She looked like she had when she had been in the tub. Within the stalk, she was withered and dead, and her branch arms that reached skyward bled dirt from the shucks of her wrists. It was the boy's mother.

She didn't look down toward the child at her root base. Instead she, like all the others, stared skyward at the lone star. Sunday moved closer and saw next to her there was a smaller stalk, and he recognized him as the mute boy's little brother.

They were here. In this field.

The boy looked at Sunday. He knew what the child wanted.

He reached out with the key, and he held it out toward her like a lantern. He held it in front of the woman's face, and he saw her eyes. She lowered her stalk head, and her eyes were drawn to the light. To the new light.

As she stared into it, the stalks began to fall away from her. The key radiated around them, and Sunday saw the little brother was also staring up at the key light.

A moment later, there was a flashing brilliance, and Sunday closed his eyes in its glow, and he felt the key shoot forth a blast that seemed to shoot all around them.

When Sunday opened his eyes again, he saw the mother standing there. The little mute boy looked up at her, tears on his translucent cheeks.

* * *

The boy saw her. And he was not sure it was her. Not the real her. Because he had been fooled by the One many times before. And He had used his mother to lure and trick the child.

He was on his knees and hesitant to reach out.

"Charbel," she said. It was *his* name. A name he had not heard in so long.

She reached out and pulled him in and she smelled as she did when she was alive.

He remembered then their time together. And he was so sorry for what he had done with the baby. She held him, and she told him it was OK, and they both wept. A moment later, his little brother stepped toward him, and he joined in their huddled hug in the middle of the hell fields.

* * *

Sunday looked around them. There were others now coming to life around them. Huddling closer to see the key.

As they neared and kneeled, Sunday watched as they began to fade. They turned transparent, as was the boy, but then he watched as their bodies began to turn to light, like they had become filtered sunlight and were being pulled skyward toward the single star.

He looked down at the boy.

His mother and the little brother were also fading, but he was not.

The mute boy held onto them as long as he could.

* * *

"It's Ok," she said to him as he clung tightly to her. She smiled and collected his little brother in her arms. And they both transformed into the light.

No. No. Please stay.

But the little mute boy was left alone, holding nothing.

He called after her, but she was gone, and he couldn't go with her.

He looked to the man and he felt the tears rolling down his face.

"I don't know where they're going," he said. "Why I can't go."

He reached out for the man. And the man held him there, as the boy wept, in the field of sorrows.

CHAPTER XXXIII

The key had shown John Sunday her pain. He had seen her face twisted into an eternal scream. And he was determined to stop it.

The boy led him toward the mountains. After what had happened in the fields, the key light in his hand began to flicker. It sputtered out some, like a gasping candle, and Sunday returned it to his vest pocket, unsure if it needed to recharge or was simply spent. He wondered if there would be any light left when they reached their destination.

The boy had said they headed toward a dark place and he was terrified of what they would find there. He had said that he had only ever known the fields, and that is where Mara had woken him. She had told him where to go, but he had never been deeper into the pit and was not certain what came next.

They walked for some time through the valley of darkness. As they did, the winds howled, and it grew colder. The root branches swayed and crackled in the sky.

"But the mountains and the caves," said the boy, as if picking up the conversation hours later, "that is for sinners."

"Sinners?" Sunday asked. *Sinner?* What crime could Kat have committed he wondered. What sin would she have done that would have led her to such suffering?   Kat was twice as good as he was. If he, with his stack of sins was still able to be forgiven enough to wield the key, then why couldn't Kat also be forgiven? Why couldn't all the others? Why were they all here in this place?

Is this really all there is?

Then he wondered. Wondered if there was something she *had* done that he didn't know about. Perhaps before they met. A secret she held that had damned her to this place. He wondered then if he really knew her at all or if the person he loved was a charlatan.

Am I doubting her?

Then he remembered their fights. And their screaming. Her cold hatred toward him that had left him alone. Divorced and drunk. She never understood him. Never understood who he was. Not when he really needed her the most. To help him with what he had done. What he had to do. Killing was a burden for him. Didn't she understand that? And what did she do? She left.

She never understood. She only judged him. Like she was better than him. Didn't she see? He had to kill because there was evil, true evil crafted by men, and somebody had to stop it. All he ever needed was for her to be there for him.

Maybe that was her punishment. Leaving him.

But why wasn't she with Mara? Why weren't they together? Why hadn't Mara tried to save her? Her own mother?

Did Mara just leave her own mother to suffer? Perhaps the sinner was *Mara*. Leaving Kat behind. Wouldn't that then become Mara's sin? Betrayal?

As they moved deeper, he wasn't sure if he was going up or going down or forwards or backwards. He felt his way along the rock wall, wondering if they were straying off the path. As the wind howled and the darkness overhead swirled, he felt the coldness closing in on him. It was a gnawing cold, that felt like it was taking small bites out of his flesh.

Was it true what the boy had said? That they were all damned? Had God truly abandoned them? Was being evil no different from being good?

Was there even a God at all?

Or maybe Mara was the *true* child of God, and therefore *truly* uninterested in what happened to humans.

What am I doing? Why am I here? Why am I bothering for either one of them? Traversing hell to get to them. Maybe he should just turn around…

Go back.

What am I doing?

Just leave them.

The cold was hurting now. His right arm felt like it was going numb. He reached over with his left to wake it, but when he touched it, the other arm felt crunchy and cold and dead.

He pulled the key, and in its very faint glow, he saw them.

He was covered in a crawling swarm of some kind of fly. They were fat and black, and as they landed, they unfurled a scorpion-like tail that inserted into his flesh and began to suck. He tried to swat them off, but they were all over him. Then he knew. It wasn't the cold that had been biting. They were feeding on his flesh, devouring him. He shone the light around and saw the boy's face and arms were covered as well. They were feasting on them.

And he didn't care.

Fuck it. He was going to let them devour him.

And everyone could cease to be for all he cared. Him. Them. Everyone.

He heard their sucking sounds on his flesh, and he stopped walking and sat against a rock. He realized then it was not a rock, but the remains of a human, sucked dry. He sat in a field of their black, withered flesh. And again, he didn't care. In the fading key light, he watched as the flies laid their eggs in him, and he saw their larvae swimming beneath his skin.

Yes. Lay your eggs inside me.

He didn't have the strength to go any farther. The boy sat across from him, his face completely covered in flies. They crawled in his mouth, in his ears, and then the child toppled and fell over.

It was then he thought he saw something. A faint light moving up the path toward them. He tried to wipe the flies from his remaining eye, but his vision was blurred by their filth.

In his blindness, he felt someone next to him. Someone touching him in the low light. At first, he thought it was the boy. But then he heard the voice of a woman.

"Hello John," she said.

That voice. I know that voice.

He tried to wipe the flies from his face so he could see her. But both arms were heavy now, and he was so weak.

"What…what's happening…" he said, but even his lips didn't seem to be moving. He couldn't hear any words coming out.

"You're safe," she said. "It's Ok."

"Kat…" he said, but it came out like a long exhale.

"No," the woman answered. "It's me…Sasha."

With that, John Sunday shot up, and he was fully awake but still blind as he struggled to wipe the flies from his face.

Sasha!

"Shhh, it's Ok. I'm here. You're safe," she said.

He wiped some of the smear away from his one good eye, and he peaked out, and there she was. The woman who had cared for him in the bunker.

She was still a blur, but she was not harmed. Not hurt. She was…

Alive.

He looked around.

He was no longer in the pit. No longer in the valley. He was back. In the bunker. With her and she was caring for him again.

He tried to speak, but he couldn't get his mouth to form the words.

He looked around the green tiled room. He could again smell the stale air. See the faint low light. Feel the cold.

He looked to her...and then down at himself. Oh God. He was back in the bed. Back in the bunker. His arms and legs withered and wilted.

How could he be back? How could he be in this place again? What was happening?

"Almost done," she said as she continued to massage lotion into his skin. "Then you'll be all clean. Good to go."

Please.

He tried to say it, but he couldn't speak. Couldn't tell her, "You have to leave. You're not safe here. They're coming for you."

She paused what she was doing and looked at him like she knew he was trying to say something.

"What?" she asked.

Men. Coming. To kill you.

He was starting to fade. He was weak again. Exhausted.

He reached for the key beneath the vest but couldn't feel it there anymore. It was just his bare skin.

Where is it?

Then he realized they were not alone in the room. There in the shadows of the wall he saw the green tiles shutter and ripple.

Next to the opening, stood a man watching from the shadows.

He had a beard, but the side of his face was concave, as if he'd been crushed by something heavy. He wore scrubs with a name tag. Sunday said the name out loud.

"Yusef."

From beyond the tiled wall, he heard the boy calling out for him in the darkness.

He knew he had to return. Knew he was just a visitor here. Knew that Kat was still out there.

"What?" Sasha said.

He was fading. Sinking lower into the bed until it felt like he was part of the mattress. Sasha was drifting farther away from him. He was leaving her.

"What did you say?" she said.

He tried to tell her…

He's there. In the shadows. Watching you.

But he couldn't. Couldn't tell her that the man she loved was standing right next to her, watching her, clinging to her because she was all the hope he had left.

And with that, Sunday was pulled into the mattress, swallowed by its fabric and he fell back through the darkness.

He woke on the ground in the dark valley. He quickly sat up and was still clutching the key and it radiated a little glow through his fist so that he could see the capillaries in his skin. He quickly checked his body for insects but saw none. They were still out there though, their wings flapping just beyond the halo of the key light. The boy was sleeping on the ground next to him beneath the light from the key. He too was bug-free.

Sunday shook him gently, and the boy rolled over and looked at him.

"Are we safe?" the mute boy asked in Sunday's mind.

"Yes," Sunday said. "I think so."

CHAPTER XXXIV

Longinus came to the hell fields.

And he saw that many of the bodies were missing. It was as if some of them had been scooped out, plucked from their roots, and what was left was an empty crater.

As he passed the rows, the thousands that remained wailed and called out to him, weeping.

They were all awake now.

They reached out to him as he passed, with their bone branch fingers, and called out for the key.

"Please. Sir. Please…"

Longinus reached a hill and stared out across the fields. He wanted to set the fields on fire, burn them all, just so they would suffer. Watch them go up in flames, just because they were alive again with hope. He wanted to take that from them because his had been extinguished long ago.

But he had no way to light a fire. Ironic, that in hell, one couldn't find a flame.

So, he moved on, had to leave them. Perhaps it was better this way. To be aware of their plight now, to realize they were trapped, and to have no escape from it. And at this thought, he smiled.

Eventually he came to the rail and decided to make time and climbed on top of it. From there he ran on the rail-top, beneath him the millions in the hell fields still crying out to Him.

* * *

Sunday still had no idea how the key worked, and it seemed to be losing its power the deeper they went. It was now a meager glow. He didn't know if it ran on some kind of cosmic battery that needed to sit idle and recharge or if there was a limited power supply and at some point, the key would just die.

As they crossed a ridge, his attention shifted. In the distance, was a vast, dark mountain chain. It was alien just in size, far larger and higher than any mountains he'd ever seen on Earth. All around it, were violent bursts of lightning. Lightning like he'd never seen before. It swirled and spiraled and shot out of the slopes and summits and into the dark, reticulated roots in the clouds. The roots carried the bursts upward still, like synapses traveling through a neural network.

"This is it," the child said as they stood on the ridge.

Sunday nodded, but he was still in shock at its sheer size. They were going to climb *this*? The Himalayas would have been easier.

They crossed into the valley of the great peaks.

"This place," the boy said, "is not what it seems."

"What does that mean?"

"The hell you see here, is not theirs. Their hell is within."

Sunday wasn't sure what that meant. But as they neared the mountains, he saw then it was not made of rock. The mountains were giant piles of bodies, merged and congealed, woven together so that they were connected to each other. Beyond the bodies on the surface, were hundreds more stacked as deep as he could see. Their flesh formed a vast skin sediment across the surface. Their faces were still twitching as electrical pulses tingled within the bodies, before random bursts of lightning shot from the side of the mountain and into the sky.

"Where do we go now?" Sunday asked.

The child looked up at him and smiled.

"To see the priest."

CHAPTER XXXV

Ephesus
74 CE

Cornelius had long since given up on the quest to find the centurion and the key. He was far too old now to be traversing land and sea in search of a ghost. Besides his vision had gotten so bad, most days he could barely find himself.

He had returned to preaching the way and had hoped it would earn him enough redemption to overcome the sins of his youth, the sins of his old age.

But then the ghost appeared in his doorway.

"I've come to collect the debt," the man said as he stepped out of the rain and crossed the threshold.

Cornelius had been about to leave the church for the evening when he saw him standing there. The centurion's face was blurred by Cornelius' poor vision, but his silhouette still looked big and strong. Stronger than him.

Cornelius nodded and instead just sat back down in one of the chairs. He could see the outline of the centurion's sword there at his hip, and he was close enough that he could smell the rain on the leather hilt. He knew. Knew it was his time.

"I know there is nothing I can say to you to take away what I have done," Cornelius said.

The centurion stepped closer, but Cornelius' eyes were too clouded to see what face he now wore.

"You're right."

"The key," Cornelius said as he heard the man draw his sword.

"What of it?"

"Do you carry it on you?"

"I do."

"I know you owe me nothing, but I have searched for it, and for you, for many years. May I…at least see it?"

The centurion reached into a pouch on his hip and retrieved it. He held it out.

"May I touch it?"

"The last time I let a follower of the way hold the key, it left me blind," the centurion answered.

Cornelius nodded.

"You and I are not so different. I joined the legion when I was fourteen," Cornelius said. "Just a child. But I was anxious to serve, to escape my father, to avenge our losses in the Teutoburg Forest. When I served in Germania, we laid waste to the Marsi tribe. We went village to village, fifty miles round, murdering every single person. Men, women, children. We locked many in their temple and burned it down with them still screaming inside. I killed babies when I was but a baby myself. Then, one day, the other men forced me to rape a girl. I lost my own virginity by raping a virgin child, while men with swords watched and cheered. And when I was done, I had to kill her." He paused and wiped the tears from his face. "And I still see her face."

"Is this supposed to sway my sword?" the centurion said.

"Nay," he said as he wiped the tears. "I just wish to say to you that what I did to your wife, to you, I knew no better. I had become an animal. And I thought what I did, was the way. But then you came back. And I saw you could return. And I thought, perhaps I too could be reborn. So, I came upon the way. And if I could speak to that boy who did what he did that night in your home, to sway his hand and his heart, I would do so."

"Do all of you talk so much?"

With that, the blade entered Cornelius' chest and pierced the other side. He gasped and tasted blood and felt the metal lodged near his lung. He toppled from the bench and the centurion kneeled next to him on the stone floor and pressed something cold into his palm.

The key.

"Here," the centurion said. "Let us both see where you go now."

The centurion closed Cornelius' fingers around the key, and though near blind, his eyes filled with a blinding white light.

When the light cleared, he was in a cold, dark cave. The cold burrowed deep into his skin and he heard the winds howling outside.

But as he tried to move, he realized he was trapped. In ice! Locked in a frozen tomb. He couldn't move! As he stared out, he could make out the silhouette of the centurion standing on the other side of the ice, staring in at him. The centurion leaned in closer and Cornelius could see he was smiling.

Then he felt the warmth of the glowing key that he had held in his hand fade away, and he felt the key being removed from his palm and he was alone in his icy tomb except for a voice he heard inside his head. It was very deep and pushed away all other thoughts.

"**All ways end here. The Lord you worship, is me.**"

CHAPTER XXXVI

The child led John Sunday through the mountains.

The priest? Why?

"How do you know where you're going?" Sunday asked as he noticed a woman within the mountainside. She was sleeping beneath the surface but stirred as if they were trapesing through her bedroom at midnight.

"When she woke me, she showed me the way and the way to come," the boy said.

"Yeah? So how does this end?" he asked.

"That part has not been written," he said. "But no matter what, it will end."

"She didn't tell you if we make it?"

"We do. And we do not. There are all possibilities here. This is a place of God and of no God. Which we are in now, I do not know."

Sunday shook his head. The kid spoke in the same kind of parables as Mara. Couldn't he just get a straight answer?

He followed the boy up the path through the mountains of bodies. As they made their way, the summits of the mountain peaks towered high above their heads, until they were no longer visible in the dark root sky.

They walked for some time, the lightning firing around them, until they made it to a rise and the boy looked at him.

"From here, we climb."

Sunday nodded, although he knew what that meant. They were going to scale a slope not of rock, but of flesh.

He pressed his hands against the side of the mountain and his fingertips sank into the surface like he had punctured a bloated body. It held his grip, and as they climbed, his hands were coated in death and the mountain stunk of rot. The steeper it became, the more he was forced to put his hands down into, sinking his fingers deep until they gripped bone so he could grab onto something solid to pull himself higher.

The mountain of dead became more putrid, and when the stench had overwhelmed him, he leaned over and puked up the already meager contents of his stomach. Sunday wiped his mouth on his sleeve and began climbing again, but as he did, there was a brief series of crackling sparks next to him and a burst of lightning shot out of the side of the mountain a few feet away. The blast knocked him off and he slid down the slope, trying to catch himself, but the bodies were slick as grease. He was sliding faster, picking up speed, and was going to fall completely away from the mountain when he was able to jam his arm into the side and he caught hold of a bone. He jerked to a sudden stop and pain radiated through his shoulder socket. He caught his breath, and as he climbed back up, he saw the face of the person he had grabbed hold off. The man within stirred and looked out at him, as if he were staring at some strange alien that had just landed on top of his world.

Sunday pulled himself back up toward the boy and assessed the mountainside again. Lightning shot across the surface and toward the sky like electric veins, and he wondered if he would be fried to a crisp first or just fall off the mountain to his death. His skin tingled and the hairs on his arms stood up. A half second later there was the crackling sound from the bodies again and there was another blinding flash of plasma. This time he was ready, and he held tight to the bone, as the lightning exploded from the surface not five feet away from him.

They continued upward, until finally they came near the peak. The bodies here were fresher. Below the dark swirling root clouds, Sunday saw the rail line was here, threading over the mountain peaks, and there were still bodies on it as it disappeared into the distance. Bodies fell off the line and toppled to the piles below, and apparently this was how the mountains had been born.

They walked until the boy came to a fresh mound of dead and he kneeled and started to roll and push a body away. Sunday helped, and they had to peel away a fleshy web that had grown between a dozen or so of the bodies, until they saw him there just beneath the surface.

Sunday gasped. There he was. He still called him Priest, more as a joke than anything. His flesh was leeching into the mountain. Father Simon was dead and rotten, but his eyelids still twitched as swirls of electricity moved beneath his pale, bloated corpse.

What had he done to deserve this? This man of God. A man who as long as Sunday had known had tried to do the right thing. Now he was trapped here like all the others, his deeds on earth no salvation from the God he praised.

Sunday looked over at the boy.

"What do we do?" he asked.

The boy pointed to Sunday's vest pocket and with that he pulled out the key. It was cold and dead and he shook it like it was a flashlight with stale batteries, but nothing happened.

He remembered the boy's words: *their hell is within.*

Sunday sat next to the priest and his rank corpse twitched, and he wondered if his friend was dead. Or was he still in there? Seeing something? What was his hell?

There had to be a way to take him from this place. But he didn't know how.

He thought then to ask for help. The concept was hard enough with people. It was even harder to ask from an indifferent wizard.

He looked down at the key in his hand.

"Please," he said.

The key laid dormant a moment and then began to glow in his palm. Charged by its simmer, he continued.

"Show me. The way."

And with that the key radiated even more, until the light in his hand was so blinding he had to close his eyes.

* * *

As Longinus ran the rail, he saw the beam.

In the distance. A burst of light that radiated. The only light in hell.

It was a light he knew. A light that had blinded him…twice.

And he knew where they were.

CHAPTER XXXVII

When Sunday opened his eyes again, the white light was fading. When color returned to his eyes, he realized he was sitting in a church pew. He looked around, trying to figure where he was. It was a church he'd never been in before, never seen before with gray stone columns and dark pews. In front of him was an altar and wooden alcove, with a giant crucifix of Christ looming overhead. It felt cold, and smelt old, and the chandeliers above produced a low, glowing light.

As he sat in the pew, he heard footsteps on the marble floor.

A man came up behind him. He was younger, and thinner, his face hard to make out in the low light, but Sunday still recognized him.

"I'm sorry," the priest said in Polish. "The church is closed."

Sunday couldn't help but smile. Somehow, he understood what had just been said, even though he'd never spoken a word of the language before in his life.

"I think I'm here," he answered fluently in Polish, "for a confession."

"Well, as I said, it's a little late for that."

"The confession isn't for me," Sunday said.

"Who then?"

"You, Father Simon."

The priest leaned in and looked him over. As he came out of the shadows, Sunday could see the priest's young face was more defined, even handsome. The weight that he would bear later in life had yet to age him even more than his years.

"Who are you?" the priest asked.

"This is going to sound crazy, but I think I've been sent here to help you."

"Me? How so?"

"You've done something. Something that troubles you?"

"Haven't we all, brother?" said the priest.

"No. This is something…something I think I've been sent to help you with."

"Sent? By whom? The communists?" the priest said as his eyes narrowed.

"Who?"

"Look, I don't know who you are, or what you want. But you come here, dressed like this, like some soldier, and you threaten me?"

"I'm here to help you."

"I don't want your help." He gestured toward the church doors. "Please. Before I call the authorities."

Sunday slowly nodded. He stood, and the priest followed him down the aisle. The priest opened one of the heavy wooden doors, swung it wide, and waited for Sunday to step outside.

"What you've done," Sunday said as he stepped past the priest, "I think we need to make right."

"My salvation, is my business." With that he slammed the church door closed, and Sunday was left alone on the sidewalk.

Snow fell from the night sky and accumulated in dirty piles on the sides of the streets. He could feel the cold, feel the snowflakes landing on his face. He looked around, trying to figure out where he was.

A streetcar lurched past. In the streetlights he saw a stone niche on either side of the church doors. One contained a large statue of a man holding a book, the other a statue of a saint gripping two keys.

There was a coffee shop across from the church. He crossed the street and stepped inside and shook off the cold. The man behind the counter paid him no attention and Sunday spotted a newspaper sitting on top of a table. He picked it up looking for some clue as to where he was.

But the date caught his eye.

January 17, 1989.

It wasn't a question of where he was. It was a question of *when.*

He lowered the newspaper. This wasn't just some dream he'd stepped into. This wasn't just the priest's version of hell. This was the priest's *life.* And he had entered it.

The key wasn't just a way between worlds. It was also a gate between time. That's how he had seen Sasha. That's how he was here now.

Possibilities?

That's what the kid had said.

There are all possibilities here.

Is that what was happening on the mountain? Was the priest re-living his life? Or at least this part of it? Was there something about this time? This place? This moment?

Trapped in a hell of his own creation?

Sunday looked out the coffee shop window at the church across the street.

What did you do?

"You want something?" the clerk asked in Polish from behind the counter.

"Yes," Sunday answered. He tossed the newspaper back on the table and stepped back out into the cold.

* * *

Father Simon checked the lock on the church door again. He wondered if the crazy man with one eye, dressed in a Kevlar vest, was going to storm back inside carrying a bomb strapped to his chest. Some communist nut-job looking to take down the church or send a message that they were in charge, and not the Polish pope.

Who was he? Talking to me about salvation. Me?

He picked up a box of hymnals and Bibles and walked back down the aisle, checking the pews to make sure there was no one else left. From there, he threaded the narrow stairs to the dimly lit basement, and as he did, he was almost certain he heard the faint whine of a kitten.

* * *

Sunday walked around the side of the church, searching for a way in. There was a side door, but it was locked. He moved back to the front of the church and looked around. Because of the cold, or the hour, there was no one else on the street but there were lights on in the nearby apartments. The lock on the front doors was heavy duty. He didn't have a way to pick it, and if he knocked the lock, someone might hear.

He looked at the heavy wooden doors and then to the statue tucked in the stone recesses next to it. It was a statue of Peter who held two keys in his hand.

Sunday wondered and reached into his vest pocket and pulled out the key. Could it, somehow, unlock the door? Or somehow move him to the other side? He held the key in his hand and closed his eyes and thought of the place he'd just been. Thought of the inside of the church. Maybe somehow it would take him there.

And when he opened his eyes…he was still standing there on the sidewalk in the snow.

He looked again at the heavy lock. A lock on a church door had always struck him as strange. That the house of God would close. That there were treasures inside that thieves could pilfer that were more important to protect than a place where prayers could be uttered at all hours of the night.

As he held the key, he looked down and saw he could see through the skin of his own hand. He could see the bones and veins, clear as if he'd stuck it into an X-ray machine. He moved the key close to the door and as it neared it glowed brighter, and in its light the heavy mahogany door turned translucent. He could see the latch of the handle *on the other side* of the door. He slowly reached his other hand through the opening, through the wood, and turned the heavy deadbolt knob.

He pulled his hand back through the wood and as the key light faded, so did the transparency of his hand. He tried the handle again and this time the door swung open.

The church aisles were empty, and Sunday checked his corners, and saw no one in the wings. He strolled the empty church and paused at a side corridor. Somewhere, down the stairs, there was a faint whine. He stepped down the stairs, down a long narrow hall with low light.

Voices were coming from an open door farther down the dimly lit hall, and he tucked into the shadows and listened. He heard the priest talking inside one of the rooms.

"How is this child possessed Father?" he heard the priest ask.

Sunday couldn't tell who the priest was talking to, and he couldn't make out the response.

He leaned forward to hear better, but then there was shouting and Father Simon was pushed out into the hallway by another priest and the door slammed shut.

He watched as Father Simon stood in the hallway and contemplated for a moment. What had happened on the other side of that door? The younger priest stood outside, perhaps wondering whether he should push his way back inside and face whoever was in that room.

The priest raised his fist up to bang on the door, but instead, slowly lowered his hand. He was not the big, heavy man he would become. He was just a thin, young man who perhaps didn't think he had the strength to make a difference in this fight.

Sunday realized that whatever was on the other side of that door was why he was here. He stepped from the shadows, and as he did the priest turned, frightened.

"What are you…"

"Let me help you," Sunday said as he moved quickly past the priest and kicked open the door.

When he did, he saw a priest standing over a naked boy tied to a metal bed frame in the dimly lit room. The other priest stood over him and held a blood-caked cross. The boy was emaciated and weak, his eyes wide with terror.

"WHO are you?!" shouted the priest, but as he did, his face transformed beneath the dim bulb. What stood now in the room was no longer a man.

The holes sin his pockmarked face opened and closed, each like a breathing mouth. Within were small maggots that wriggled free from the holes and fell to the ground. The smell of rot filled the room.

Father Simon stood in the doorway. But the priest was no longer young. He was as he had been when Sunday had last seen him. Father Simon looked at Sunday, as if wondering what he was doing here, how he was here, and then looked past him to the holey priest.

"There is no salvation!" hissed the priest hissed as he turned the bloody cross around and held it like a knife.

Father Simon reached down and pulled a Bible from a cardboard box near the door. He pushed past

Sunday and took the Bible and raised it in the air like he was going to strike the priest down with it.

Instead he shouted, "Tremble in fear, Satan, you enemy of the faith, you foe of the human race, you root of all evil and vice! Christ the Lord brings your plans to nothing! Fear Him!"

The demon gave a sly little smile.

"I'm not the devil. Just a man."

With that, the demon priest lunged forward with incredible speed and tackled Father Simon. He landed and sat on top of him like a bird at roost. The demon priest raised the cross into the air, and Sunday grabbed hold of his arm to try and stop him, but he was incredibly strong. The priest plunged the cross down into Father Simon's chest with a sickening thwack.

Father Simon sputtered and gasped. Sunday struggled to pull the priest off, and he reached into his vest and grabbed hold of the key. Before he could use it, the demon hurled him across the room and the key fell on the floor near Father Simon.

"Get the key!" Sunday shouted to him.

Father Simon wrapped his beefy knuckles around the key. As he did, the key radiated in his fist and sent out a shock wave so strong it blew the demon priest clear across the room, shaking even the boy tied to the metal bed.

Father Simon, slowly, painfully rose to his feet. He and Sunday moved over the demon priest as he shuffled to get back on his feet. As Father Simon neared with the key, the demon cowered back into the corner.

"Strike terror Lord," the priest gasped, his lungs wheezing. "Into the beast laying waste your vineyard. I cast you out, along with every Satanic power of the enemy, every specter from hell, in the name of our Lord Jesus Christ. For it is He who commands you!"

With that Simon brought the key closer until the demon priest was consumed in its light. Everywhere the light touched, the demon disintegrated. An arm, then a leg, then the left side of his chest, as if he were being eaten by some giant, invisible mouth. He screamed and hissed, until the light evaporated his throat, and he was gone.

When it was done, Father Simon looked at his chest, at the cross wedged near his heart. He collapsed and Sunday caught him and helped him gently to the ground. The wound was too close to the priest's heart, and if Sunday pulled out the cross, he would bleed freely. He could do nothing for him.

"This…you…how are you here?" Father Simon asked.

"I don't know. The key brought me," Sunday said as he nodded toward it.

"I," he gasped. "I remember…drowning. Dying."

"Yes," Sunday said.

"So, is this real?"

"I, I don't know what that is anymore."

"Is there a heaven?"

"I don't know."

Father Simon patted Sunday's hand.

"I…I think there is," the priest said.

A moment later, he took one last breath and Sunday watched his friend die. Sunday clutched Father Simon's hand as he closed his eyes one last time. The priest was a good man. A man who deserved to go to a heaven. Instead, he just laid there on the floor, going nowhere.

Sunday looked around the basement, wondering what would happen next. If the room around him would just disappear and cease to exist with the dreamer's death, and even Sunday would be gone. Instead, the priest just lay there on the floor, bleeding out. Sunday picked up the key and put it back in his vest pocket. He walked over to the bed and undid the binds on the terrified boy.

"It's alright," Sunday said. "You're free."

The boy looked up at him, eyes wide, deeply afraid. And Sunday couldn't blame him.

Sunday again raised the key and brought it down against the metal bedframe. With that, the room wobbled around him, and when the gate opened in the basement wall, he stepped through it.

Once he crossed, he was again on the mountaintop standing next to the priest. The body though was being ejected from the mountain like it was being spit out. As the body emerged, the priest's clothes and body were wet as if he had just drowned.

The priest's eyelids rolled back, and his dead pupils twitched as if he was still seeing something. Dreaming something. Sunday didn't know then if he'd made any difference at all, or if the world he'd just seen was playing out all over again in the dead man's mind.

A few seconds later, Sunday watched in horror as the priest's eyes withered away and his skin quickly decayed and rolled off him until he was just a pile of bones.

What's happening to him?

The boy ran across the mountaintop toward Sunday. He was excited as he spoke in Sunday's mind.

"Come! Hurry!" he said as he turned to leave again. "I've found her!"

"Who?" Sunday said as he quickly followed him.

Not twenty feet away, the boy stopped and pointed to a body trapped in the side of the mountain. Sunday neared and examined her face.

It was not who he had hoped it would be.

It was the junkie.

CHAPTER XXXVIII

Somewhere in Israel
Seven Years After Event

They drove slowly along the snow highway, and even with the windows rolled up, Lincoln was freezing. He'd dressed for the heat, not the cold. He'd had to slow the car to a near crawl, because the headlights didn't work, and he couldn't see more than ten feet ahead of him in the darkness. The Mercedes slowly snaked around stalled cars, their rooftops now piled high with the snow. They were losing time.

How could there be snow if the planet was roasting? But he knew the answer, he just didn't want to accept it. As he drove, he heard the crickets outside again, even over the diesel engine. They were out there, chirping in what had hours earlier just been sun scorched desert. But it wasn't crickets, was it? No. He knew what it was. It was the things from the hell winter that had returned, and they were out there talking. Talking about him. Talking about stopping the car that was now only cruising along at a mere ten miles an hour.

The Indian man reached into the backseat and held his mother's hand as if he too remembered the sound of the crickets.

"Can you use a gun?" Lincoln asked.

The Hindu shook his head. "I can. But I won't."

Yeah, that's what Lincoln figured. Lincoln pulled the .38 back out of the glove box and placed it in his lap. He hadn't fired a gun since he'd been a kid. Out with his dad.

His dad.

He remembered him again and his heart suddenly filled with a wave of memories…of love. The moments they shared together when he was growing up. Their father-son talks on the way to school. His father, the school janitor, so proud of his son.

His father there hugging him as Lincoln went off to college, but Lincoln still coming home to see his father because he was his best friend. That time when he brought home Carol Connors and they had such a nice evening together and he thought he and Carol Connors just might get married.

Them going sailing together. He had such a sudden, strange flood of memories of his father, of their time together, and then he just as suddenly missed him all over again.

What happened to his father?

He couldn't remember. Had he made it through the hell winter? Why hadn't he thought through all this before? Why didn't he head back home to the U-S to try and see if he was still alive? To save him?

Why was his father's memory suddenly so strong and fresh in his heart?

He noticed then that the old lady in the backseat was smiling.

"What?" he asked as he looked at her in the rear-view mirror.

She spoke then in Hindi. Lincoln looked to Dharma to translate.

"She says you have found your father again."

Lincoln turned and looked at her. "How does she know that?"

She spoke again.

"She says that the way you take now is the one you were always supposed to take. The one where your heart is free of sin."

"What does that mean?"

The Indian woman just smiled.

Lincoln was about to ask her again, but he spotted something on the highway. Something near one of the still cars. Something that moved.

It's dark. Your eyes are playing tricks on you.

He pushed down on the gas a little more, but as they passed a dead car, that something unseen landed with a thud on top of the Mercedes. The old lady in the backseat cried out, as the roof sagged from the thing's weight.

Jesus, it's on the roof.

Whatever it was shifted around up there, and the metal groaned, and Lincoln thought to shoot a hole through the roof. Instead, he floored it, speeding blindly through the darkness.

"Buckle up!"

The Indian pulled his seatbelt around and he gripped the dashboard, bracing for an impact they couldn't see coming. Lincoln watched the speedometer, twenty, twenty-five, thirty. The old diesel dragged on the pick-up.

He was cruising along at forty, this thing still on the roof, not knowing if he was going to plow into something and wreck the car. Without it they'd have to *walk* in the darkness.

The thought caused him to suddenly slam on the brake, and the thing on the roof shifted its weight and then something dark flew over the hood and landed ten feet in front of the bumper. Lincoln couldn't see what it was, but it slowly rose, a dark shadow in front of them. The old lady in the backseat gasped.

Lincoln spun the wheel and floored it again, as fast as the old diesel could go, which wasn't much, and he swerved onto the median. The snow wildly spun the back tires, but they were driving. Sliding. Driving, sliding. As they sped away, they left the shadow in the rearview mirror, as they drove on into the darkness.

CHAPTER XXXIX

Sunday once more stepped through the gate made by the key and when his vision returned, he stood in the darkness of an empty street in a rundown neighborhood. Trash choked the gutters and it stunk faintly of sewage. In the distance was the silhouette of a dark city, and somewhere farther down the street he heard screams and the barking and yapping of dogs.

As the key light faded to a dull halo, he realized he was standing in front of a squat concrete block house. A gunshot rang out somewhere in the distance and he wanted to get off the street quickly, so he moved toward the house. He peered through a side window, but it was too dark to see if anyone was inside. The screams were getting closer and he heard the clicking of bone heels at the end of the street. Somewhere out there, he knew, were the hell spiders.

To his surprise the door was unlocked and he quickly stepped inside. There was no one in the front room, and he moved quickly through to a kitchen, toward a back door. He opened it and saw it led to a small, empty, walled-in backyard. As he turned back through the dark kitchen, he slipped on something, but couldn't make out much in the darkness, and was afraid if he pulled the key to look, the light would attract whatever was outside.

The house was sparse and small, one empty bedroom where it looked like several people slept. The only other door, at the end of the hall, was closed. He slowly opened it and saw a woman on the floor, slumped against a bathtub. She was wearing a robe, her head back and eyes closed, a needle and syringe stuck in her arm.

He kneeled and checked her pulse, and as he did, her head flopped forward and she stared at him, her eyes still rolled back in her head so that only the whites were visible. Still, he knew who she was. The junkie.

"Are they there?" she whispered as her pupils fell into place again.

"Who?" he asked.

"My family," the junkie said as she noticed the needle stuck in her arm.

"I don't know."

She plucked the needle from her vein like it was suddenly a nuisance and then offered him the syringe.

He shook his head. "Uh, no."

"Then why are you here?" she said, annoyed.

"To help you."

"Help me what?"

"Help—save you."

"Save me?" she laughed, and slowly started to stand. She almost toppled, but he caught her. She was cold as ice and shook off his arm and reached out for a lighter on the sink counter. She flicked it and used the flame to see him better.

"You want to see something?" she said in the fire-light.

He wasn't sure that he did. Regardless, she released the lighter and stumbled out of the bathroom and into the darkness of the house. He followed, wondering what he was supposed to do here. How he was supposed to help her. In the kitchen she flicked the lighter again and then he saw.

"Shhh," she said. "They're sleeping."

There were bodies leaned up by the kitchen sink. Three children. An older man. They'd been stabbed to death and their eyes were all open, as if they'd been sitting there waiting for him the whole time. Sunday knew now what he'd slipped on earlier. Their blood.

"This is what she did," the junkie whispered, as if someone else was listening.

"Who?"

"Grandma."

She lit a candle on the kitchen table. "I came home. And they were all playing outside. Having fun. Laughing. I smelled grandma's cooking. But then— she started killing them all. Grandma doesn't like laughter."

He stared at the bodies. The old woman had done this? Killed a grown man and three children?

The junkie moved toward the back door. "Hurry. We have to lock up. Get the front. We don't want anything else to get in."

Sunday moved back through the darkness and locked the front door, and with the halo from the candlelight in the kitchen, it looked like someone was sitting in a chair in the shadows of the next room. He neared the corner to look, but before he could, he realized the junkie was standing behind him. He turned and a half-second later, she leapt toward him. She moved like lightning and plunged the syringe into the side of his neck, and he felt it release its warm contents inside him. He shoved her back, and even though she was much smaller, she didn't budge.

"There's no escape," she said.

A heatwave was coursing through his veins. His arms and legs were becoming rigid and he slowly slid to the floor.

"What…did…you…"

But even the words weren't coming.

She whistled as she retrieved the candle. The tune he knew.

"Row, row your boat. Merrily, merrily, merrily life is but a dream."

She came back and looked at him in the candlelight. As she did, her face began to change. The flesh was smearing, changing.

"What…what…dichoo gi me?" he asked again, drool pouring out of his mouth.

She placed the candle on a table and then reached down and picked him up like she was lifting a small dog and placed him on the couch. He sat there, helpless, staring up at her in the candlelight. She smiled seductively and opened the front of her robe. And there, beneath her breasts, was the tattoo of a string of lilies.

"Lilly?" he said, his head and thoughts smearing into the upholstery.

"Miss me?" she said, as she moved closer. She pushed away the tail of her robe and straddled him and she stroked his hair and caressed the front of his chest.

"Don't you see?" she said as she leaned in and whispered near his ear. "We're all connected here."

He felt her reach down and pull out his cock and he had no strength to stop her.

"We can be anything," she said as she fondled him. "Do anything." she whispered. She leaned back and her eyes were dark as pitch as she slid on top of him and began to grind slowly. "We are everything."

She rode him and he had no power to stop her. Her breath was heavy, and she reeked of death.

There was something else here with him. Someone watching from the next room. Someone there, sitting in a rocking chair. Watching. He could feel it probing his mind. Rocking back and forth in the chair.

He remembered this place. Remembered he needed to get out.

He suddenly surged with everything he had, and yelled, and pushed the woman off him and she toppled onto the table and onto the floor.

"What the hell?" she said as she looked up at him.

Sunday stormed into the side room. In the flickering light of the candle in the next room, he saw her sitting there in the chair. The grandmother.

The naked junkie scurried behind him like a spider. She was screaming, the sound drifting in and out, and he fumbled in his pocket, his hand feeling like it wasn't even there as he tried to grab the key from his bulletproof vest. He couldn't get his fingers to follow his instructions.

The grandmother stood, and he moved away from her. Suddenly she was standing inches away from him, as if time had skipped, and she pinned him against the wall as he fumbled for the key.

"We are the beginning and the end," the grandmother hissed.

The junkie girl crawled on all fours like a spider at his feet. The room twisted and contorted around him. He wrapped his numb fingers around the key and pulled it out and showed it to them like it was a cross to ward vampires. But like them, the key was cold, dark and dead.

"Pleesh…" he said, his mouth unable to form the words. "God."

The key radiated a second, but then the light snapped and fizzled. The grandmother held him there as the junkie grabbed hold of his ankles and her hands began to merge into his legs. She was becoming him.

"No," he gasped, but he could feel her now in his body. Trying to take over. Trying to take control. He closed his eyes as she dragged him down to the floor, the skin of her fingertips oozing into the flesh of his ankles. She was consuming him.

Then, he remembered Kat's face. Sitting across from him as they dined together in Egypt. She wore a sundress, and she smiled at him, as she was beautiful.

"Please," he mumbled again.

With that the key radiated, and his numb fingers began to warm, and then the key burst forth in a shockwave of bright light that rattled his organs. He heard screaming and he opened his eyes, and squinted in the light, and saw them both.

Dozens of small hell spiders crawled out of the pores on the junkie's skin and evaporated in the light. The grandmother dropped to her knees as a large spider detached from her spine and shriveled in the burning light. It smoked and squealed on the floor.

When it was done, and the room stunk of seared flesh, the junkie and grandmother looked to each other. The junkie helped her grandmother to her feet and they held each other in the light of the key. They both turned to Sunday and smiled, and with that, they too faded in the light of the key and were gone.

When the light had dimmed, Sunday felt the numbness from the drugs recede and he was stone cold sober again.

The walls around him were fading, and as he stepped through one of the walls, he was standing back on top of the mountain. Lightning swirled around him one more and the bodies toppled from the sky. Across the way, he saw the boy. But he was not alone.

Hovering over the child was a man—a Roman centurion with a sword.

* * *

Longinus jumped off the rail and landed on his feet, the flesh of the mountain absorbing the impact. He landed near a child. *A living child*. The boy started to run, but Longinus grabbed him by the back of his little blue winter coat and spun him around and saw the child had a deformed face, half of it caved in and missing.

"Where is he?" Longinus barked.

The child opened and closed his mouth but said nothing.

"Where?!" Longinus said as he pulled his sword from its sheath. He brought the blade under the child's chin as the boy's pale eyes went wide. "You've been freed. How?"

The boy didn't answer.

"No matter," Longinus said as he pressed the tip of the sword into the child's neck. "Return to your cell."

With that, he slid the blade under the child's chin and through his throat.

Longinus looked up and saw the man he sought suddenly appear on the mountain. He tossed the dead boy to the ground, and when he did, the bodies of the mountain reached up and pulled him down into them.

* * *

As the boy was dragged into the mountain, Sunday heard him trying to cry. He was trying to say something in Sunday's mind.

"Forg…" the boy sputtered on broken breaths. "Me."

The boy in the blue winter coat grabbed at the air as if drowning, trying not to be pulled into the dead, until he was swallowed into the mountain and was mute once more.

The centurion was only twenty feet away, and Sunday watched as he wiped the bloody blade on his chest. He knew then that he was going to kill this man and it would bring him joy. He had no weapon. Only the key. He reached into his pocket and pulled it out.

Please.

But it did nothing in his hand. The centurion was coming closer.

Sunday returned the key to his pocket and looked around for something to fight with.

He was unarmed and he knew the odds. He'd have to run.

There! Across the surface about thirty feet away, he spotted the decayed bones of the priest. He raced for the pile as the centurion swung with the blade, and Sunday dodged and rolled as the edge swiped through the air near his head. A half second later, the centurion swung the blade back around as Sunday came to his feet. He was too close, too close, and the blade sliced his back, slashing the bulletproof vest.

The impact knocked Sunday to his knees. He tried to rise, but before he could, the centurion kicked him, and he fell again. He scrambled back to his feet, but the centurion was too close.

He turned to face him as the centurion charged and Sunday jumped at the same time, and the two collided. Sunday grabbed hold of the sword arm, holding it down with everything he had. But it wasn't enough. The centurion was far stronger, or he was just too weak. The centurion head-butted Sunday, and his world started to spin. It was all his attacker needed.

The centurion jabbed forward with the sword, and in a second, he ran the blade up and under the bulletproof vest.

Sunday sputtered and gasped as the blade sliced into his ribcage. The sword pushed deeper still, and Sunday cried out.

He was pinned on the end of the man's blade.

The centurion moved closer so he could ram the sword the rest of the way through. Sunday grasped the man's scarred face and jammed his thumbs into his attacker's eyes. The man pressed the blade deeper still and Sunday screamed out in pain. They were both locked together, each man pinned to the other.

One of the centurion's pupils burst beneath Sunday's thumbnail. Now the centurion cried out in pain, and with it, he pulled the blade and retreated a few feet. Sunday collapsed as the blood poured out of his gut. He struggled to his feet. The centurion groped at his bloody socket as Sunday limped away.

He reached the pile of bones and fell into it, sifting through it until he found what he was looking for. He plucked the priest's femur from the pile and stood as the centurion returned within striking range. The Roman's eye wept blood, and yet he smiled.

"We're all blind here."

He brought the sword down again, and Sunday swung the femur up to desperately block the blade. The sword landed with a thud and the bone splintered, but the fat priest's femur held.

Sunday tried to sweep the centurion's leg, but even half-blind, the centurion anticipated the move. He followed it with a knee strike into Sunday's chest, slamming it into his open wound.

The blow knocked the wind out of him, and Sunday backed away. He tightened his grip on the bone club as they each sized each other up again on the mountaintop. This was it. He was going to live or die here.

The centurion charged. He brought the blade high, and Sunday countered, but the centurion reigned down with a flurry of blows. Sunday used the bone to block, but the centurion kicked him in the chest and he nearly toppled over the edge of the mountain. He caught himself from falling as the centurion brought the sword down again and again until the priest's femur shattered and Sunday was knocked to his knees.

He kneeled there on the side of the mountain. He had nowhere to go. Nothing left to fight with.

The centurion hovered over him and brought the tip of the sword inches from Sunday's face.

"There's no escape here," the centurion said.

Sunday tasted the iron in his mouth. He was drowning in his own fluids. The centurion reached out with a blood-stained hand.

"Give me the key."

Sunday considered reaching into his vest pouch, pulling it out, giving it to him. Because he'd been beaten. Because God had not saved him.

There was crackling on the mountaintop and he knew the sound. Sunday rolled quickly away, and a second later, there was a blinding blast as a bolt of lightning struck a few feet away. The centurion was knocked backward and seemed to be on fire.

Sunday couldn't tell because he'd been blown off the side of the mountain. He fell through the air until he landed hard on the bodies some thirty feet below. The ridge was sloped and as he landed, he tumbled backward. He tried to grab at something to stop his roll, but it was too late. He slipped over the edge again and was rolling down the side of the mountain.

He bounced off the bodies, his head slamming into their bones, and he was building speed. He tried to slow, tried to stop rolling by sticking out his legs, but instead it just sprang him farther off the ground. He landed again, upright enough to at least drag his feet, and he was now sliding down the mountain like a snow skier, and it was then he saw he was headed toward another abyss, this one a vast, dark ravine.

He couldn't slow enough and he flew over the edge into the darkness. He fell some fifty feet, until he landed hard on something spongy and wet. The impact knocked the breath out of him, and more blood burst from his wound. He tried to lift his head, but he was too dizzy, too weak and losing too much blood.

He had no idea where he was or where he'd landed, but he could tell he was moving. He groaned as he reached into his pocket, his hands shaking, and he felt for the key. He couldn't find it, and he worried it had fallen out on the way down the mountain and was lost to him forever. His cold fingers searched more, and then finally he felt it there, and he pulled it out and closed his eyes and it glowed a little in his hands.

He groaned again as he held up the light and saw his body drenched in blood. He'd fallen into some kind of river of pale red froth. He rolled to the side and saw tusks of hair protruding from the mound on which he landed. Maggots crawled over the masses and he gagged as he realized he was floating on a vast mat of congealed bodies that appeared to have been devoured and were now just pulpy mess.

All around him were the high walls of a canyon. He continued drifting, his head getting heavier. He fell back onto the bloat, his last thought before he passed out was that he was going wherever this river took him.

* * *

Longinus stood and patted out the remainder of the fire that was still burning on his clothes. He approached the edge of the mountain and watched as the man with the key rolled down the side. He saw him roll off the edge and then land in the river.

And he knew where the river went.

CHAPTER XXXX

Israel
Seven Years After Event

Lincoln hoped they were a couple hundred miles outside of Jerusalem, but he really had no idea. He could make out more Israeli license plates on the cars as he passed, but in the snow and the darkness, he couldn't read the signs overhead very well so he didn't know if he was heading to Jerusalem or driving past it.

On top of that, they were running low on gas. That meant they'd have to stop. And in this darkness, with those things clicking out there again, that was a fill-up he'd been hoping to avoid. They were back down to only about ten miles an hour, and God knows if they'd passed a hundred of those things, and they'd been following behind them like a parade for the last hour.

He chugged along until he felt they were going slightly uphill and then pulled over and parked at the peak so they could roll down the other side.

"Alright!" he said, and he took the keys out and ran around to the trunk, slipping in the snow as he did.

He put the key in the trunk lock, and scanned quickly around him, but couldn't see anything out there in the darkness.

He popped the trunk and grabbed a five gallon can of gas. He pulled it out, unscrewed the fuel cap, and then sloshed the gas all over the side of the car and his shoes before finally getting it in the hole.

The chirping was getting louder. Beyond that, somewhere down the snow road, he heard clicking. Like bones on pavement.

"Come on," he said to the gas can.

Five gallons wasn't much. He needed to get more fuel in there because he didn't want to repeat this whole process again in another hundred miles. He finished the last of the can and tossed it back in the trunk and quickly grabbed another. He repeated the process, a little cleaner this time, but it didn't matter because he already stunk of diesel.

As he filled the tank, he heard something behind him. Close. Something trudging snow.

What he wouldn't give for a flashlight or a flare.

He lifted the can higher to speed it along, and then realized whatever it was out there, was maybe twenty feet away from him. He pulled the nozzle out, chucked the can, and then ran back to the front seat. As he did, he ran smack into something.

"Jesus!" Lincoln shouted.

It was a woman. Small, middle-aged, wrapped in blankets to keep herself warm. She looked at him and spoke slowly in a stilted Russian accent.

"Please. Sir."

She pulled out her young son who had been hiding behind her. Even in the low light, Lincoln could see the boy's eyes were missing from his skull.

"Please. A ride?" the woman said.

Somewhere in the darkness, Lincoln heard the bone heels coming faster. His yell had alerted them.

"Get in!" he said as he opened the passenger seat and shoved them inside.

He climbed in the driver's seat as someone else in the darkness screamed.

"Please!!" a man yelled.

Lincoln popped the brake and began the slow roll down the hill.

"Wait!" the woman cried. "Please! My husband."

"Papa!!!" the boy cried out the window.

But they were already rolling down the hill, and Lincoln wasn't about to brake. Not with whatever it was out there.

"We can't stop!" he shouted.

But the boy was screaming, and the mother wailing.

"Please! Please stop!"

Lincoln looked over at the Indian, who just nodded. He slammed on the brake, and the engine knocked and came to a stop again, and he got out.

"Help push!" he shouted to Dharma.

A few seconds later they heard someone crunching snow, running toward them. They saw him emerge from the snow fog, but chasing him was some huge, shadowed thing, far bigger than Lincoln had ever seen before.

"Go! Go!" the man shouted as he ran.

Lincoln and Dharma started pushing the car down the hill as the running man took a flying leap and dove into the back of the open trunk of the Mercedes. They were still on enough of a slope, and they got the car to roll, but the creature was closing in on them.

Lincoln hopped in the driver's seat, and popped the clutch, and the engine started.

"Come on!" he shouted to Dharma.

The Indian climbed in the passenger seat, but as he tried to close the door, a bone tentacle wrapped around the side of the car door. Lincoln floored it, but the creature was clinging to the car and slowing them down.

The Indian slammed the door again and again on the creature's bone spur, but it did nothing. Lincoln pulled the .38 around and pressed the barrel hard against the bone and pulled the trigger, the echo of the gun deafening inside the cabin of the car. A chunk of bone blew off and landed in the floorboard. Free of its grip, the car lurched, and they were moving again.

Ten miles per hour.

Fifteen.

"Come on!" Lincoln said as he floored it, the old diesel already giving what it could. The creature was closing in behind them, the thuds of its limbs growing louder.

Twenty.

The creature knocked the rear of the car, and the little car almost flew off the snow highway. Lincoln spun the wheel back, flooring it the whole time, wondering if he was going to flood the engine and they'd just stall again and roll to a stop.

Twenty-five.

He couldn't see anything, and even twenty-five miles per hour was too fast on this slick dark road. He figured they'd just drive right off the edge of some unseen cliff and save the thing behind them the trouble.

Thirty.

With that, the thuds behind them grew more distant. Until they were cruising along, and Lincoln expected to slam into some stalled car in the darkness.

"Left!" the boy called out from the backseat.

Lincoln looked back at the blind boy.

"Do as he says!" the woman said.

Lincoln turned the wheel left, and as he did, they narrowly missed a stalled big rig sitting dead in the dark. They passed its ghostly silhouette, and Lincoln wondered how in God's name the blind kid knew it was there.

As they cleared the truck, the little boy leaned close to the cushion in the backseat.

"Papa?"

From the trunk, they heard a muffled voice.

"I am here," he said.

* * *

A half hour later, Lincoln let off on the gas pedal and was cruising now at about twenty miles an hour.

They hadn't seen any more creatures, but in the darkness, he still had no idea where he was going.

The boy called out again. "Right!"

Lincoln did as he was told, and this time they passed a line of dead cars.

"This is your exit," the boy said, pointing to an overhead sign shrouded in the snow. Lincoln slowed the car and got off on the ramp.

"How does he know to do that?" Lincoln asked.

"He hears the voice," said his mother.

"What voice?" Lincoln said.

"Do you not hear it?" asked the mother.

"No," Lincoln said as he looked to Dharma. "Do you hear a voice?"

"Yes. She told me that we would find each other on the road," Dharma said.

"She?" said the Russian woman. "For me it is a man."

Dharma nodded and smiled.

"What about you?" Lincoln said to the blind boy in the backseat. "Who do you hear?"

"I hear her," the boy said. "The one you seek. Eve."

Lincoln turned around and looked at him.

"And she says to tell you now that you are on the right road," the blind boy said.

The little boy pointed off into the distance. Lincoln saw it. There was a city out there in the cold. And there were lights.

CHAPTER XXXXI

Sunday woke on a shore. It was raining, and he winced in pain as he rolled over. When he opened his eye, he realized he was closer to the root sky, and the rain was cold, muddy water dripping from the stalks.

His hands trembled as he pulled out the key and used the low glow of its light. With it, he could see the falling rain was blood red. He pulled apart his vest and lifted his shirt to look at his wound. It was starting to fester, and he was bleeding freely.

He lowered the shirt and looked at the river from where he'd come. The rafts of flesh continued drifting on, but as he followed it, he saw large roots along the shore that fed into the water like giant pipes.

Beyond the falling red rain, he heard the howling of the wind from beyond the muddy berm just over-head. He groaned, and rolled, and groaned again as he pushed himself to stand. He stood and thought he was going to fall over and tried to catch his breath, but he knew. Knew it would soon be over.

He stumbled up and over the berm and saw them. The roots from the river ran over the hill and into a vast tangled briar. Trapped within the fibrous fingers were humans. At first, he thought they were trapped in the roots, until he saw it was all just flesh—the roots themselves moving and made of skin—and the people merged and writhing within its skin grip. Their eyes were closed but they were all screaming out in pain and weeping.

The roots latched into each body, and had inserted into their flesh like a probe, and their bellies were fat and bloated and pregnant. Even the men. The roots crawled over the bodies like tentacles, and he watched as one inserted itself into a woman's belly. A crackling noise caught his attention and he shone the key light closer. With it, he saw a man's stomach distend and roll, and then there was a pushing of his gut, and from between his legs emerged a hell spider about a foot wide. The spider was an amalgam of human body parts, its legs made of long fingers, its spine arched and pale. Within its hide were newt-like eyes and toothy mouths that opened and closed.

Sunday backed away as the spider scurried quickly toward him. He shone the light near it, and its little mouths let out a squeal, and it backed away from the light. He shone the light across the briar and saw there were hundreds of bloated bellies within the roots, and as far as he could see, spiders were emerging from the carcass bowels.

This is where the spiders were born.

He moved along the path and held the halo of the key light close. Spiders fell at his feet and scurried toward him, their fingers and arms stretched wide to attack. When they neared the ring of light, they retreated, but still followed him.

In the distance there was a dark and broken temple and he moved slowly, painfully, over the rocky path toward it. As he neared, he saw someone standing next to one of the columns watching him in return. They moved down the path and whoever it was, was coming toward him.

He had nowhere to go. The root bodies and hell spiders choked the path behind him. He was already dragging, his feet stumbling, and he didn't have enough left in him to fight. He kept pushing himself forward, trying to wind himself up for a fight, until he slipped in a puddle of filth. He tried to pick himself up again, but he just laid there as the blood rain fell on him.

He was beaten.

In the screaming of the bodies trapped in the briar, he passed out.

* * *

He woke, startled, in the low light of the key glowing in his palm. He sat up quickly, too quickly, and winced in pain. His shirt and vest had been removed and he looked down at the wound in his side. It had been stitched shut.

He was out of the rain and inside the temple. Outside, beyond the stone columns, he could see the roots feeding in the distance and hear the low wail of their screams.

There was movement in the shadows, and he brought the key light around and saw someone sitting near the base of a column. He retreated, painfully, and from the shadows he heard a woman's voice.

"It's Ok," she said. She stood, and slowly approached. As she neared the light, he could see her face.

"Do you remember me?" she asked.

He brought the key closer and examined her face. Even though her hair was matted and wet with red mud, and her cheeks were dirty, she was still pretty. It came to him then.

"You—the woman. At the hospital. In Israel," he said.

"My name is Ayelet," she said as she kneeled near him. It was then he could see that she was naked and pregnant.

"You were losing a lot of blood," she said as she nodded toward his stitches.

"Why are you here?" he asked.

"I saw the child before I died. She came to me. Held my hand, but I didn't recognize her. I heard her though, whispering to me. Telling me to repent for my sins. Telling me to wake. And *I did*. And the hell roots fell out of me."

She scooted closer and showed him her hands to indicate she was not going to hurt him, and then leaned in and checked his stitches. "I knew you would come. Come to save us. She told me what we have to do."

"What's that?"

"Take you to her."

He scooted up into a sitting position and winced as he did.

"You know where she is?" he said.

"Yes."

"Where?"

"Not far now," she said. "The rails, the river, the roots—they all lead to the same place. They all feed the One and that is where she, where they both are."

"Kat?"

Ayelet nodded.

He slowly, painfully started to stand and she helped him to his feet. He looked again at the wound in his side to check that it held.

"Where did you find thread?" he asked.

"Don't ask," she said.

CHAPTER XXXXII

Jerusalem
Seven Years Since Event

As they drove, they passed more people. Dozens of them, running toward the illuminated city.

As Lincoln drove, some of them clamored and banged on the windows, begging for a ride, but he couldn't fit any more people in the car. He knew now they were headed toward the Old City, and as they neared, the road was too clogged with people to drive.

"From here, we run," said Dharma.

Lincoln stopped the car and jumped out. He opened the passenger door and the Russian mother held the book in her hands and she handed it to him as she got out. She then nodded toward the trunk.

"Right," Lincoln said. He grabbed the keys and unlocked the trunk, and a bearded man in his forties was lying there curled up near the spare tires and gas cans.

"Thank you, sir," he said as he climbed out of the trunk, "for stopping car."

He then moved past Lincoln and ran toward his wife and blind child and hugged them both.

Lincoln looked to Dharma who had picked up his mother from the backseat and now carried her on his back.

"Now what?" Lincoln said.

"We hurry. The things come."

Lincoln and the others raced with the crowd through the darkness. They reached the walls of the Old City and followed the masses toward the Damascus Gate. Soldiers stood guard outside and were closing the iron bars to the entrance.

"Wait!" Lincoln shouted.

He turned and yelled to the group that was lagging. "Hurry!"

Lincoln made it to the gate and stood at the threshold and guided the others through as the soldiers closed the iron bars behind them.

He stepped through the stone gatehouse and into the Old City. There were thousands of people on the cobblestone streets. Men, women, children. They continued walking and he saw there were Africans, Asians, Europeans. Indians and Islanders, and Jews and Christians and Muslims. There were Buddhist monks and Hindu sadhus with painted faces and Sikhs in turbines. There were African tribal elders and Chinese Taoist priests.

"How many are here?" he asked Dharma.

"144,000." Dharma said.

Lincoln figured he should have known that number. He remembered it from his Sunday school classes:

Then I heard the number of those who were sealed: 144,000.

"So, where do we go now?" Lincoln said.

Dharma nodded to the book. "Home."

CHAPTER XXXXIII

John Sunday had given her his shirt and he wore only the vest, and together they followed the stone path until its end. They climbed over the flesh roots, each helping the other as they did. The bodies within screamed and moaned as spiders scurried over them, but as he held the key, the roots and the spiders retreated from the light.

She was far along in her pregnancy and he was careful to help her. As they reached a root ledge, he could see the branches still went skyward like giant stalks.

"What now?" he said.

"We climb," she answered as she clutched her belly in pain.

"How long?" he asked as he gestured toward her stomach.

"I don't know. Time here has no clock."

"What happens after you give birth?" he said.

"I get pregnant again. And again. Forever."

He tucked the key into the pouch of the vest and followed her as they climbed the roots until even the flesh-mountains were far below.

The higher they climbed, the colder it became, until his fingers struggled to grip the twisted bones and bodies trapped in the roots. Below was the vastness of the alien landscape, and the roots draped over the land like tentacles. This high up the branches illuminated deep within from the bursts of lightning below, and they climbed until they emerged through a cloud of solid ice.

Here they stood on an ice land supported in the sky by the thick roots below. Ayelet disembarked, and Sunday looked out across the ice that was both under his feet and frozen in tiers above his head.

What also drew his attention was that twisted within the ice, locked among the frozen roots, were more bodies stacked in rows—one in front of the other—hundreds deep.

"All of the bodies below are connected. They're re-living their suffering over and over again," Ayelet said as they crossed the frozen field. "When they die on Earth, they return. A birth on Earth comes only from the previous one's death, and each is bridled to the previous one's sins. They are all trapped in a life of sin that they live over and over."

She stopped and pointed toward the mouth of an ice cavern. "She's this way," Ayelet said as she gestured.

"How do you know all this?" he asked, shivering.

"We are all connected." She pointed to the roots that continued even through the layers of ice above his head. "Everything feeds into the One and He feeds on us."

He followed her past more trapped bodies, past countless faces with their eyes frozen open. Behind each body, he could see there were many more. Body after body stacked like suits in a closet.

"Why are they here?" he asked.

"The ones here have betrayed their covenant with God. Betrayed the way."

John shook his head. He couldn't understand what sin Kat would have committed to be in a place like this. She'd betrayed the way? She hadn't betrayed anyone.

They reached the cave and he peered inside. It was too dark to see and so he pulled the key to light their way. It faintly glowed, enough to cast dark shadows as they walked past more bodies. After a few minutes, Ayelet stopped and pointed.

"There," she said.

John followed her finger and saw a woman's body trapped in the ice. He ran toward her and slid as he approached. She was bound in her frozen chamber but looked as she had been in life. Her hair and face were locked in place, her fingers frozen, yet reaching out as if still wanting to be touched. Her eyes were open, but cold and dead, and within the ice there were still roots that clung to her. Behind her, were stacks of more people, body after body frozen in the ice like a hall of mirrors.

He banged on the ice with his fists, but it made no difference.

Ayelet came up behind him.

"How?" he asked, his voice cracking. "How do I get her out?"

"You can't," Ayelet said. "Those here are kept closest to the One. She is special. This place is reserved for those he treasures. The ones below are recycled. Re-used. They play out their lives over and over. Their little stories, their dreams, their nightmares. Each one born of the next, and so each holds to a little hope that the next dreamer will create a better place beyond this world. But these...these bodies have no hope. They just end."

He brought the key closer to the ice, and he could see more of her cold, blue skin.

"No," he said under his breath. He placed his palm on the ice and in this cold, dark place, he closed his eyes and prayed.

"Please," he said.

With that the key burst into a brilliant light and he was awash in white.

When he opened his eyes again, he was no longer in the cave. Instead he was standing in a hospital hallway. A female nurse pushed a man in a wheelchair down the hallway next to him.

"Where am I?" he asked her.

The nurse kept moving as if she didn't see him.

"Hey!" he said, but she kept going until she pushed a button on a set of double doors and kept moving down the hall.

The key pulsed in his palm. He moved down the hall, checking rooms, looking for some clue as to why he was here. *If* she was here. He passed a room where an old woman was watching television. Bill Clinton was on the screen testifying about Monica Lewinsky.

It's happened again.

Farther down the hallway he spotted a little girl, no more than six years old, sitting by herself and playing with a doll. He moved slowly toward her, not sure if she could see him and he'd frighten her. He sat down next to her and she didn't even look over at him. Her face was familiar. Her cheeks, rounder and puffier, but he knew. Knew who she was.

"Kat," he said out loud.

The little girl kept playing with her doll.

"Kat, it's me. Can you hear me?"

She brought the doll close to her chest and held her, and it was obvious to him now that she'd been crying. She wiped her eyes and looked down the hallway toward a door.

"Hey," he said again.

The door across the hall opened, and a doctor and a woman stepped out. John recognized her as well. It was Kat's mother, although far younger than he'd ever known her. Still her hair was a mess and her eyes were puffy. She approached and Kat looked up at her.

"Are you ready?" her mother said, and it was obvious to him now that she too had been crying.

Kat slowly nodded. She slid off the orange plastic chair and reached up and held her mother's hand. Sunday followed behind them. They paused for a moment outside the room as if both were afraid of what lurked on the other side of the door.

Sunday knew where he was headed before he stepped into the room. The tears gave it away. When he followed them into the room, he saw him lying in the hospital bed. Her father. He was bone thin, his face and eyes hollowed by cancer or chemo or both. Only a few strands of hair were left on his head.

Kat looked to her mother and her mother nodded and told her it was OK.

Kat was hesitant. Sunday knew why. He'd heard this story before. Her father had been on chemo for some time, but his body was covered in painful sores, and for months Kat was prevented from even giving her father a hug. From touching him. He was a ghost to her long before he ever died.

Kat moved slowly toward him, and her father could barely keep his eyes open. He rolled over, his eyes trying to focus on her. He tried to say something, but what came out was incoherent.

Kat crawled in bed with him as if he were about to read her a story, and she snuggled up next to her father. She looked at him and stroked his unshaven face. He seemed coherent enough to know what was happening because tears rolled down his cheeks. Whatever drugs they had him on hadn't taken that part of him away. He knew who she was. Knew he wouldn't see her again.

Sunday realized then he was doing more than just watching what was happening here. He was also *feeling*. Feeling everyone in this room. Their thoughts. Their grief. His heart felt this unbearable weight, this sticking fear festered in his gut.

Kat laid there for some time next to her father.

And Sunday stayed with her the whole time.

Eventually, an alarm beeped, and the nurses ran into the room. Kat was scooted off the bed, and then back toward the hall. She paused at the door and looked back at her father as they worked on him, but her mother tried to drag her by her hand out of the room. She planted her feet and held firm.

Her father spoke again to his daughter, and this time he was understood.

"Leave," he said, his voice no more than a hoarse whisper.

She nodded, and relented to her father's request, and cried as her mother pulled her out into the hallway.

Sunday watched as the nurses went to work and a doctor ran in to help, but there was nothing left to do. Her father seized in the bed, and went stiff, and then relaxed. As he did, he stared at Sunday. Her father smiled at him, as if he saw him there, and then spoke one last time.

"Buh-leave."

When her father was gone, Sunday stepped into the hall, but Kat and her mother were gone. The hallway had changed as well, like it had suddenly been remodeled. He looked down both ends of the corridor. He was still in a hospital, but perhaps a different floor. Or perhaps, a different hospital?

There was screaming and nurses ran into a room farther down the corridor. He followed them into the room and saw Kat was in labor. This was not when she had given birth before, when he had delivered Mara. This was the time that the baby had died, the one he never saw. She screamed and the baby was delivered and now he saw it too small, and blue, and dead. She asked to hold it, and then screamed at them, and they let her.

He felt her then. Felt her horrible pain, her deep sadness as she looked at what she had failed to make.

She hated him, and he felt that, and he understood why. He knew he'd been selfish, and he'd left her here to deal with this so he could go off and try and kill himself.

He tried again to speak to her.

"Kat?"

He repeated her name, but she couldn't hear him. She just sat there, rocking the baby, sobbing. He reached out to hold her hand, but his fingers passed right through hers and then through the bed itself.

The nurses took the baby from her and she curled up in a ball in the bed and held herself. He clutched the key and whispered a prayer, but when he opened his eyes again, she was still there, still aching.

There was a flicker in the overhead lights and the room around him suddenly reset and then she was back in the fetal position, pushing and straining. She gave birth again, and then again, over and over. She screamed, and was handed the baby once more, and no matter what he did as he stood next to her, there was nothing he could do to change it.

"What do you want!" he screamed toward the ceiling.

As if answering, the key radiated in his hand and the light engulfed him. The walls of the hospital room turned transparent revealing one vast hall that extended in both directions, and as he stared from end to end, he saw a million different versions of Kat.

He watched her as she was checking out of the hospital. With each step he took forward in the hall, he was moving forward through her time. He looked down the opposite direction of the corridor and there were the nurses rushing her into the hospital room to give birth. He saw her collapse while checking-in at the nurse's station. Farther beyond that, he saw them making love in the bedroom, the ghost curtains flapping in the windows. And he saw himself choking her in her sleep. Events that had happened years earlier.

Somewhere along this path, he thought, was her sin. Somewhere was what she had done to deserve hell. And he would have to find a way to stop it.

He decided to watch it all. He turned and stepped through her past as if he were just moving past rooms in a hallway. With each passing room, she grew younger and younger. There she was in Egypt when they'd first met. There she was studying in college. With other boys. Trying marijuana. He saw her in Catholic school, studying, praying. Going to church. Believing the word, believing the way. He heard her in the pews, praying to both God and to her father in heaven.

He followed her all the way through to her beginning and saw her being born in yet another hospital room. Faintly visible on the other side of the hospital wall was the blur of another room that he could not pass through. There sat an old woman in a rocking chair in the front room of a house. The woman took her final breaths and slumped forward in her chair and when she died, Kat was born.

He saw nothing along her journey that seemed to warrant damnation. Marijuana? Sex in college? Really?

He stepped from the room of her birth and this time ran forward. As he did, her timeline sped past him. Soon he was watching her pack for Jordan, and then harness up and he was in the cave with her again. He saw her imprisoned in Egypt and watched as she was bound. He saw her being impregnated and eventually, he was with her again on the journey through Lebanon, in the snow, during the hell crossing.

He watched as she fled on the boat, and he was tied to the mast, and then they made it to Patmos. She read to him as he was tied to the bed in a tiny cell.

Eve appeared in the cell with her, and Kat took the key, and then her timeline and the room went dark. He stepped into the darkness of this room, and he ascended the steps toward a torchlight, and he saw Kat talking to an obese red-haired man dressed as a Caesar reclining on purple pillows in a Roman colosseum.

He neared and heard them speaking.

"Please," she said. "Let him go."

The Caesar looked up at John and smiled as he approached. The Caesar *could see him*.

"Give me my life, with him," she said. "And then when it's over, and I die, I will be yours."

John stepped forward. "No," he said. But the Caesar waived a hand, and John could speak no more.

The Caesar smiled. "So be it."

John tried to grab hold of Kat, but he passed through her again, and then she was back running through the tunnel.

The Caesar looked to him and smiled. "Her sin, was loving you."

Sunday chased after her, and he shouted for her, but it did no good. He couldn't get her to see or hear him.

He watched them together then as he moved forward through their lives together on the island with

Mara. He watched both Kat and Mara be crucified, and then when she was dead, the key radiated again in his hand.

And then, what was a lifetime later, he was standing back where he had been all along, his palm pressed against the ice, Kat still sealed on the other side.

Ayelet stood next to him, talking to him as if no time had passed.

"I said," she continued, "her timeline is locked. There is no freeing her."

He slowly nodded as he stared through the ice at Kat. Trapped there. Alone. Frozen for eternity, and he realized he was crying because he could do nothing except stare at her cold grave.

Ayelet stepped closer to him. "There may be another way."

Sunday looked to her, and it was so cold, the tears had already frozen to his face.

"What way?"

CHAPTER XXXXIV

Jerusalem
Present Day

Lincoln and the others tried to navigate through the crowd outside the Dome of the Rock, but there were far too many people. They had gathered, men and women and children, and each was packed shoulder to shoulder.

The Russian family disappeared somewhere in the crowd, and as he clutched the heavy book, Lincoln tried to push his way through to the front. Dharma and his mother followed him as a Nepalese Sherpa in the crowd began shouting at him in a language Lincoln didn't understand.

"Uhāṁsaṁga pustaka cha!" he called.

He was swarmed by men and they grabbed at the book, and Lincoln tried to keep it, but the men pulled it from him, and then it was gone.

The crowd carried the book, hand over hand, and guided it toward an empty stage. No one stood officiating over the crowd. Instead a handful of young boys carried the book up on the stage and placed it on a wooden pedestal. As soon as they did, the crowd cheered.

The men who had taken the book helped Lincoln back to his feet. They smiled and patted him on the back and dusted him off. Then they hugged him.

Lincoln had no idea what was going on. And he seemed to be the only here without a clue.

The crowd around him began to sing a song he'd never heard before. It was no hymn or prayer gospel. No chant or mantra. It was like the entire human condition had swelled into a single chorus, creating both a low wailing and a simultaneous singing. A weeping and a laughing. A cry, a lament, a plea.

Lincoln didn't know how, but all these people sang together. Dharma and his mother smiled at him as they too sang. Each person was rising and falling with the notes liked there had been some lengthy dress rehearsal he had missed.

That's when he became afraid. Why did all these people know this song, and he didn't? Did that mean his name was not in the book? That the things he had done to Eve, *the things he had to do*, had counted against him. Were the things 'he had to do' just an excuse for doing wrong no matter what?

Lincoln didn't know the song.

What would happen to him because he didn't?

CHAPTER XXXXV

Ayelet led Sunday deeper into the ice cave, past rows of ice-locked bodies. She finally stopped, and pointed at a body in the wall, and Sunday approached. He held up the key, and there trapped in the ice, was a man he did not recognize. An old man, his beard gray yet frosted with ice, and he stared at him.

"Who is this?" he asked.

"His name," she said, "is Cornelius. He was a Roman centurion. He was also the first outsider to become a Christian. He spent much of his life seeking the key you now hold in your hand. He chose the way, even though he was a soldier. A sinner. Like you."

"How can he help?"

"Because," she said as she tapped on the ice, but her face suddenly went white, and she sputtered. Her eyes widened, and she gasped and started to fall. As she did, he saw why.

The centurion stood behind her, and he pulled the blade from her back.

"Return to your place," he said as the pregnant woman slid off his blade and collapsed on the cave floor.

Sunday moved toward him, but the centurion held the sword ready for t

"Do you see?" the centurion said. "Who you are? See what you have done to me?"

"I don't understand," Sunday said.

"Like me you have lived a hundred lives. You just don't remember yours."

The centurion moved forward and grabbed Sunday. He shoved him against the wall, the dead old man locked in the ice just over his shoulder.

"Let me show you," the centurion said as he nodded toward the key in Sunday's hand. "Use it."

Sunday held the key in his palm and it radiated.

"Remember to close your eyes," the centurion smiled, and with that, they were both immersed in blinding white light.

* * *

When the light dimmed, Sunday was sitting in the woods. In the distance, the sun was setting, and farther down the valley sat a villa. Men were speaking nearby. There were several soldiers leaning against the trees. *Roman* soldiers drinking bottles of wine which appeared to have come from a nearby cart stacked with similar jugs.

Where am I?

"We need to get back," slurred one of the soldiers in Latin.

Latin? I understand Latin?

"Before they see we're gone," continued the man.

"Flocci non faccio," said another. "Cornelius, what do you say?"

Sunday stared down at his hands. Beyond the key, he was also holding the neck of a jug of wine. It was if he had two hands, blurred together into one. He looked down and moved his legs. He could feel the wine in his body. He felt drunk. He was not just watching this time. He was living it.

"I say his wine is good," he heard himself say, but it was not *his* voice.

"So is his wife," said one of the men. "Who saw that?"

"Those tits! Silky udders!" said another.

The men laughed. There was more talking about what that man had, and what they did not have, and by nightfall they had decided to go back to the villa.

As Sunday stepped through the dark woods, he tried to stop himself from moving forward. He knew what he was about to do. What their plan was. He tried to speak to himself, a little voice in his own head. "*Stop*," he said. "*Don't do this.*"

The body he was in heard his pleas, and then he heard the man's thoughts dismiss such a feeble, weak notion. He could feel this man was excited. He was primed. And he wanted this.

Under the moonlight, each man pulled their swords and silently entered the house. From there, Sunday watched as the centurion stepped from the shadows. The centurion attacked, but the other soldiers quickly put him down, and they stabbed him until he lay limp on the floor.

Then a woman appeared from the shadows.

And each of the men took turns on top of her.

He tried to tell his body not to do it. He looked down and saw the woman beneath him as he pushed inside her. Her eyes wide as she begged him to stop. But he didn't. He didn't until he was done.

And then he lifted her to her feet, and drunk on wine, he took the blade and he slit her throat. He heard the centurion on the floor try to scream out, but all he could muster was a bloody gargle. Then they ended him with the jagged edge of the blade.

The soldiers around him faded away, but Sunday remained. The house was empty, except for the two dead bodies.

He watched as the dead centurion on the floor became rapidly coated in white spindles. Suddenly the dead man sat straight up and wiped the gunk from his face, and when he saw his dead wife, he stumbled over to her and screamed in the empty atrium.

He placed her body back down gently on the floor and he turned and moved toward Sunday.

"See what you did?" the centurion said as he picked up his sword from the floor. "You made me who I am. Made me what I am. If not for you, the blood of the Christ would have kept me alive, and perhaps I would have preached His word for all to hear. I could have been pure enough to wield the key thousands of years ago. I could have brought the earth back to where it belongs."

"What does that mean?" Sunday asked.

Longinus smiled. "One last vision before you die."

With that, Sunday was standing on a hill next to the centurion. The skies were dark. On top of the hill, three men had been crucified, and at their feet, were a handful of people. A small group was on their knees and weeping. The rest were Roman soldiers. Sunday knew where he was. What he was watching. The crucifixion. The centurion stepped forward with a spear. He approached one of the bodies and jabbed the tip of the spear into the man's side.

When he pulled out the spear, the fluids burst forth from Christ's side and landed on the centurion. He wiped the filth from his face.

"Surely this must be the Son of God!" the centurion spat, holding up his fluid-stained palms mockingly toward the crowd.

Sunday watched as the centurion stepped down the hill and the skies above rumbled. The ground shook and then Sunday watched as the clouds darkened. There was the sound of what seemed to be a ripping across the sky, like a rolling drum of thunder followed by the bellow of a horn. The clouds and everything around him turned blood red, and then the world was drained away of all color before it returned to normal.

"That was it," the centurion said.

"What?"

"The moment God rejected us. Tossed us from heaven. The moment He gave us to the One. Bound our worlds forever together. Because we deserved it."

Longinus moved toward him with the sword. "The key you hold unlocks that door, but to a master who is no longer home." He gestured to the small crowd on its hands and knees at the base of the hill. "Even they, the saints, the apostles, are trapped here. That is why some martyred themselves. Because they knew. Knew they had been abandoned by God and they believed it was the only way to earn His redemption." He turned and smiled. "But there is none. And now it is too late. Both worlds are ending. And when they do, all of this, was for nothing."

Sunday looked down at the key in his hand. Its light was fading. It was true. Sunday knew it. Everything he'd seen led to one inescapable conclusion: we're damned.

The centurion brought the blade up toward Sunday.

"Kneel," the centurion said.

He did as he was told, and he kneeled there at the foot of the cross. He looked up and saw the dead, bloody face of Jesus.

As he did, he heard the words of a man inside his head. A voice he'd not heard before.

"The way to me is through you."

"Perhaps for us both," the centurion said, "this death will finally be the last."

Sunday held the key in his hand, and he closed his eyes. And then there he was again with Kat, and they were dancing again under the aurora with Mara nestled between them. He held the key close, and as he did, the centurion stepped forward and Sunday felt the cold steel of the tip of the sword press against his throat.

But as the blade started to move into his jugular, Sunday grabbed hold of the centurions' wrist, and they both disappeared in a burst of white light.

* * *

Sunday was again a Roman soldier sneaking through the shadows of the centurion's house with the others. In his hand, he could see both the sword and the key, merging. As they stepped through the darkness of the home again, Longinus stepped from the shadows to attack. But as he did, Sunday clenched the key in his fist and brought it up, and there was a flash of light, and Longinus was blinded by it.

With the light there was a thundering boom and the stone pillars of the home shook and Longinus' eyes went wide. Sunday held the key high and the centurion and the drunken soldiers froze.

"See!" Sunday shouted. "See the light of God!"

The soldiers stood there awe-struck. One of the men pissed himself, and the drunk soldiers turned and fled from the house. The centurion clutched his head in pain, and closed his eyes, and dropped to his knees.

"What…what have you done?" he asked in agony.

Sunday's head began throbbing, his eyes were pulsing. His vision filled with electrical sparks like he was having a seizure. Something inside him, something inside his mind, was changing. He saw the deaths, the killings, the sins all play out in front of his eyes, but the visions began to fade like a dream he could no longer remember.

He heard Mara whisper again.

"I have cast your sin, again."

He closed his eyes, searching for the sins of his life. He could remember none. No guilt that plagued his soul.

He moved toward the centurion to help him to his feet.

"What did you do to me?" Longinus asked.

"I saved you," Sunday said. "And you saved me."

Longinus started to speak, but before he could, a woman emerged like a ghost from the shadows.

The centurion stood and watched as she approached.

"Licinia?" he asked.

The centurion dropped his sword and it clanked on the marble floor as she stepped toward him and smiled. He reached out and traced her cheek and touched her face. And he wept as he held her there in the atrium of their home.

"We have everything," she whispered to him.

Longinus smiled and embraced her again.

"Why?" Longinus asked as he turned to Sunday. "Why did you do this?"

"You know why," Sunday said. "Take me to her."

Longinus slowly nodded. He looked to Licinia and stroked her hair and wiped a few strands from her face. "You have always been my heaven."

He turned and clutched Sunday's arm, and a moment later they disappeared again in the light.

They emerged again in the ice cave. Sunday wiped the frost from the ice tomb, but the person he saw frozen on the other side was no longer Kat. It was a man he did not know.

"Where is she?" Sunday said.

"Something has changed," Longinus said. "She no longer had to be here."

"So, where is she?"

"There is only one way to find out," Longinus said. "We must go to The One."

Sunday followed the centurion out of the cave, and they resumed the climb up the roots, through multiple layers of ice. They crawled through the narrow cracks made by the roots, until they could climb no higher.

Sunday and the centurion surfaced onto a vast, barren, wind-blown landscape of dark rock. Above his head, he saw not only all the stars, but what seemed to be all the galaxies. It was as if he was looking at the entire cosmic ocean all at once.

All of it was being pulled into a giant, swirling emptiness. As he stepped off the roots, Sunday could feel it tugging at him, drawing him toward it. Around the swirling blackness, the galaxies and stars were being sucked in and ripped apart. He realized he was standing on the shore of some massive black hole, watching millions, perhaps billions of years of destruction happen all at once.

"My God," Sunday said as he stared up.

"Not quite," Longinus said.

It was then Sunday realized that the roots he had climbed had ended at the base of a vast, towering kind of tree. Instead of solid branches made of wood, the limbs radiated with pulsating colors. It was huge, like he was staring at a fibrous, pulsing, rainbowed sun.

"What is this?" Sunday asked.

"What is left of Eden," Longinus answered.

As he stared at the tree, Sunday saw a little girl step forward from the trunk. He couldn't tell if she had been standing there in front of the tree all along, camouflaged in its light, or she had emerged out of it. As she moved toward him, he knew who it was.

"Hi Daddy," Mara said. "I've been waiting for you."

"Mara!" he said as he dropped to his knees and hugged her. As he held her close, he heard another voice again inside his head. This one was dark and deep and cold.

Show me.

Sunday pulled away from Mara. The thing he had hugged was not his daughter. Her face had become translucent, as if she were still forming inside the womb.

He scrambled to get away from her.

"Who are you?" he said.

The One. The Singularity. The everything. Show me what you have brought.

Sunday looked at the key in his hand. He looked at the embryonic child in this empty, barren place, and then at the worlds being pulled into the giant black hole. It all seemed to be dying.

What do I have to lose? What does it matter?

"What happens if I don't?" he asked.

The child stared at him with its optic nerves connected to two cold, dark black stubs.

Then the world you know will be wiped from existence.

"And how does this," Sunday said as he held the key, "stop that?" He looked toward the black hole.

The key opens the door. It is your chance. To live beyond this world.

"So why don't you just take it?"

It must be your choice.

Sunday looked at the black hole. At entire worlds being devoured.

"No. This...*you* need this," he said as she watched him closely with her translucent eyes. "This is a key so you can escape."

The child smiled from lips that weren't yet fully formed.

"And you can't take it, can you?" Sunday said. "You would have done so by now." He looked at the tree. "No. This, this place...this is where *you* are trapped."

We are both trapped here.

"Then why do you make us suffer? Why not create something beautiful?"

Because you have destroyed everything beautiful ever given to you. The Mara-thing smiled. **And God has turned His back. On both of us.**

"No. There's something more. I've felt it. You want this?" Sunday said as he held up the key. "Free them. Free all of them. The ones here, the ones still on Earth."

To go where?

"Someplace better. Someplace beautiful. Someplace free. Of you."

Who are you to barter with me?

Sunday was suddenly lifted off the ground and he felt his skin begin to burn. He looked to the centurion for help, but he could offer none. Sunday's flesh bubbled on his hands and face, and then his skin was torn from his body. He hovered in the air as he was burned and skinned alive and he screamed out in pain.

No matter where you go, you will devour.

Sunday writhed in agony and he held out the key with a burnt, peeled hand and screamed.

"You will not get this key!"

The Mara-thing slowly nodded.

So be it.

Sunday dropped to the ground, and he watched as his flesh congealed and healed. The scars and burns faded away. He caught his breath, there on his hands and knees in front of the Mara thing. He looked up at her as it gestured toward the tree.

From out of the illuminated trunk, Sunday stood and watched as Mara and Kat appeared.

As they ran toward him, he could see they were as they had been. He didn't know if they were real or another figment created by this thing and he didn't care.

He pulled Kat in and held her as the winds whipped around them.

"I knew you'd come," Kat said as they held each other.

Mara watched them both. Sunday kneeled next to her, but hesitated, unsure if it was really her.

"It's Ok," Mara smiled. "It's me." She moved slowly toward him and then wrapped her arms around his neck and hugged him. It felt like her. Felt like home.

She whispered in his ear. "Ok, Daddy. I'm ready." She held out her hand.

Sunday looked to the Mara-thing that still watched and waited. Sunday turned to Longinus.

"What do I do?" Sunday asked.

"If this is all there is, then it will have to do," the centurion said.

Sunday looked again to the embryonic Mara.

The Mara-thing tilted its head as if knowing what he was going to say before he said it.

"This isn't our salvation," Sunday said. "It's yours."

He handed the key to Mara. She took it and ran back toward the Tree. She reached high and one of the illuminated branches reabsorbed the metal key into it, into an electric flowery burst, and then it was gone.

The tree then burst forth in blinding white light. The light fired across the barren land, and then shot through the roots of the tree, deep below the ice. Beneath it, Sunday could see the white light traveling through the root veins, crackling into the ice crypts, into the bodies of the frozen.

The light from the tree was blinding, and Kat and Mara huddled close to him, and they were all absorbed by the light, and then he saw no more.

CHAPTER XXXXVI

Jerusalem
Present Day

A dark cloud swirled over the Old City. People huddled together as the cold winds blew around them. Outside the gate, there was a deafening thud, and the crowd stopped singing as the earth shook beneath their feet.

With that, a little boy appeared and walked across the front wall. He sat on the edge overlooking the crowd and smiled. He acted like he was counting each of them in the crowd and then pointed up.

The soldiers on the walls overlooking the outside of the city started screaming. One shouted down to the crowd.

"They're here!"

With that, something huge slammed against the stone walls. The stone collapsed, raining men and rock into the crowd.

People screamed and trampled each other in the chaos. Lincoln watched as huge beasts, made of human flesh but far larger than any he'd seen before, crossed over the city wall. The leg of one of the beasts toppled the stone wall as it stepped into the city. He'd never seen something so huge, so out of place in his world. All he could do was stare at it, his brain trying to decipher how this thing could exist in the land of men.

Hundreds of people were being trampled around him.

Some were swooped up, and away, and carried through the air by the giant beasts. Others were stomped and crushed in to a bloody pulp.

Lincoln was knocked to the ground, and panicked people stepped on him. Dharma and his mother were there on the ground next to him. Lincoln tried to reach out and help Dharma, but all he could do was grab hold of his hand.

He was being trampled to death. A foot kicked him in the head, and he felt the world around him begin to spin. A person fell on top of him, and then another and he struggled to breathe as he was buried beneath their weight.

He closed his eyes.

It was time.

In that, he saw. He saw that he was locked in some mountain somewhere, unable to move, and all around him were ridges and peaks made of people. They too had woken, and were screaming in the abyss, crying out.

Lincoln knew then, he was going to die. He knew then, this was where he was going to go. Because there was nowhere else.

And then he heard it. Deep down. Something inside him.

It started as a single chord, like someone had plucked a string attached to his brain and heart. He heard that single note that it seemed had vibrated since the beginning of time. The single chord that set the cosmos into motion. That began existence.

He pressed his lips together and he hummed that single note. As he lay there, dying, the weight of humans crushing his lungs, his last breaths would be the song he'd waited too long to learn.

Dharma lay next to him, and he looked dead, but somehow over the screams of the crowd, Lincoln heard him whisper.

"Let there be light."

Lincoln started to close his eyes, but then in the chaos, he saw a little girl walking across the stage. She held something in her hand. It glowed.

The key?

Mara?

She moved toward the book on the stage and used the key and unlocked the binding. Suddenly there was a blast of white light that poured from its pages, and with it the creatures and the boy on the wall were devoured by the beam.

The blinding light then poured across the crowd and Lincoln was engulfed in it.

And then he heard his name…

EPILOGUE

When he opened his eyes, he stood on a hill overlooking a crystal-clear river. Tall grass swayed on either side. Far in the distance, the branches of the tree jutted skyward. In the grass he spotted a primitive ape, kneeling and drinking near the stream. It paused and looked toward him.

John Sunday heard her words drifting across the field.

And the leaves of the tree were for the healing of nations.

He'd been thinking about his father. He had not thought about him in some time. He of the Old Testament wrath. He wondered where he was. Why he had not seen him through his journey. Or perhaps he had, and he was a face he didn't recognize.

He moved back up the hill, toward the others.

And there shall be no night there; and they need no candle, neither light of the sun, for the Lord God giveth them light and they shall reign forever and ever.

They had all gathered. The priest. The mute boy and his family. The junkie and hers. Eve and Lincoln and her father. Kat's father. And all the others.

And I, John, saw these things, and heard them. And when I had heard and seen, I fell down to worship before the feet of the angel which showed me these things.

He moved closer and sat in the grass next to Kat and the dog. In the distance, was their little village. Above them the lone star was in the sky, and it cast a maroon glow across the field.

He looked to Kat and leaned in and held her hand. She smiled at him as he whispered in her ear that he loved her. Mara sat at on a rock in the middle of the field and continued the evening lesson.

"I am the Alpha and Omega. The beginning and the end. The first and the last."

As he looked at Kat, he wondered. Wondered if this place was real. Wondered what would happen to them when even this came to an end. Wondered if they could ever evolve into something better. If this place, if this time, was when it could begin anew.

None of it mattered.

He was here now.

With her.

Mara looked to her father and smiled as she finished the prayer.

The followers of the way responded then in unison.

Amen.

ACKNOWLEDGEMENTS

The end has come.

What began as a dream when I was twelve years old has now become a trilogy spanning more than a thousand pages.

Who knew that whatever I ate for dinner that night would still haunt me all these years later?

In that crazy dream (*vison?*), there was a man guiding his horse through a snow-covered wilderness. His goal—to protect a chosen child from the demons hell-bent on keeping the world in darkness. I have no idea where that imagery came from, but it evolved into John Sunday, Kat Devier and Mara.

The dream may have started the journey, but I would have been adrift in the abyss if it hadn't been for a few people to help light the way:

Jim and Gunn Loyd have been passionate supporters, constantly encouraging me that I had a great story and the talent to tell it.

Adam Hall, David Gatewood and Kevin G. Summers have been instrumental in design and editing.

Brian Shields, Nancy Alvarez, Chantal Watts, Kim Farah, Jackie Johnson and Key Jean-Michel helped me to tighten and revise.

Finally, this is a love story about a man who will do anything to protect the woman and child he loves.

And so—as always and forever—for Kris, Hannah, Harrison and Hailey.

ABOUT THE AUTHOR

James Holmes is a journalist who has been writing for television for twenty-five years. He's covered the dark side of human nature for so long he needed a fictional outlet to come to terms with where we're going as a species.

He wakes at 1:30 every morning to write and in this caffeinated haze, his literary monsters are born.

He and his wife homeschool their three children.

43623992R00172